BALLAD TALES

to dance

BALLAD TALES

AN ANTHOLOGY OF BRITISH BALLADS RETOLD

EDITED BY KEVAN MANWARING

FOREWORD BY CANDIA MCKORMACK

Illustrations by Kevan Manwaring, 2017
Cover illustration by Andy Kinnear, 2017

First published 2017
Reprinted 2022

The History Press
97 St George's Place,
Cheltenham, Gloucestershire, gl50 3qb
www.thehistorypress.co.uk

British Library Cataloguing in Publication Data.
A catalogue record for this book is available from the British Library.

isbn 978 0 7509 7055 6

Typesetting and origination by The History Press
Printed by TJ Books Limited, Padstow, Cornwall

Contents

Acknowledgements

Thank you to all the singers, collectors and listeners of these ballads.

'The Laidley Worm of Spindlestone Heugh' by Malcolm Green was previously published in *Northumberland Folk Tales* (The History Press, 2014).

All illustrations by Kevan Manwaring.

Foreword

Selkies, storms, sorcery, seduction … this is the language of the ballads that have been passed down to us from generation to generation.

The lilting rhythms of the poetry have woven their way into our psyches, enriching our appreciation of the land and giving a deeper understanding of our ancestors. There is magic all around us, of course, but it is often drowned out by the din of technology, hidden from view as we choose to watch our lives unfurl through the reflection of an ever-darkening black mirror.

There is a certain charm to the telling of tales, to the act of listening – really listening – and of retelling through song and speech, with the nuances that arise with each rendition. As music is recorded, uploaded, downloaded and shared, there is the temptation for others to create a faithful rendition – tutorials provide musical notation, lyric sites make sure you're word-perfect, there are even computer games that reward you for how closely you adhere to the original! Really, though, the 'tribute band' generation is taking its final bow and standing aside for a people who care about the art of storytelling, care about musicianship, and care about the joy of gently unravelling the cloth woven by storytellers before and creating something beautiful, entwining

old threads with new. This cloth carries the fading colours of the old, while weaving in the bright-hued yarn of the new; ever changing, with respect for what's gone before while celebrating the excitement of what's yet to come.

And so it is with this collection of tales inspired by ballads of old; I do hope you enjoy reading them as much as I ... and, should you choose to retell any of them, please do remember to weave in your own bright thread.

Candia McKormack
Singer, Inkubus Sukkubus, 2017

Introduction

A collection of ballad tales might, on the surface, seem redundant – the very term could be thought of as tautological. Surely a ballad, in essence a narrative-in-song, 'a folksong that tells a story', is a tale in itself and requires no further retelling? Well, there are indeed many fine ballads that can be listened to and enjoyed for their own sake – a good cross-section are referenced in this anthology, and either before or after reading the respective prose retelling I recommend that you check out a selection of recordings from the archives and from modern musicians. You will perhaps be surprised by the number and diversity of the versions on offer – with different lyrics, melodies, and arrangements – none of which 'break' the original, if indeed such a thing exists. There is rarely an ur-text or master copy for a ballad – even if we go by the oldest known recording, others may yet emerge. And you can guarantee that the version recorded at that precise point in time was just that – a snapshot of an ongoing process, one with deep roots and ever-growing branches.

For a ballad to be 'traditional' it is usually required to be anony-mous and of perceived antiquity, although in actuality all ballads were written by somebody, somewhere, somewhen, and many were penned in the late nineteenth and twentieth century. Indeed, contemporary folk practitioners occasionally find their own song assimilated into the folk tradition and thought of as 'trad' – a category error considered an accolade by some. David Buchan, in *The Ballad and the Folk* (1972), offers one definition of a ballad as 'a narrative song created and re-cre-ated by traditional oral method', although he recognises the problems inherent in the notion of oral tradition and is careful to nuance his

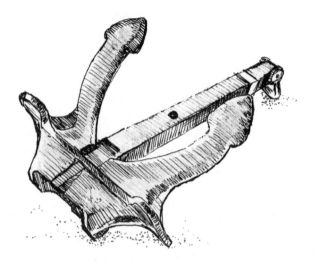

definition later into various subcategories (oral texts; oral-transitional texts; chap-transitional texts; chap texts; modern texts; and modern reproductions of these), even though he acknowledges Francis James Child's warning: 'Ballads are not like plants or insects, to be classified to a hair's breadth'. Perhaps the best approach is a practical one. As Steve Roud, author of several books on folklore and folk music, including *The New Penguin Book of English Folk Song* (co-edited with Julia Bishop in 2012), quipped in a Folk Tale Symposium held in Stroud in September 2016, 'a folk song is a song sung by a folksinger'.

I began researching folk songs, their collectors, and the nebulous processes of the oral tradition, as part of a Creative Writing PhD at the University of Leicester. The collection process can never be infallible or completely comprehensive (due to the collector's expectations, research ethics and social skills, their competency at transcribing lyrics or music accurately; the performer's memory, and other mitigating factors – the presence or absence of family members; work; illness; class; religion; ethnic and national prejudices). Something is always missed. For example, when Cecil Sharp and Maud Karpeles (leading figures in the folk-song revival of the early twentieth century) visited the tradition-bearer Jane Hicks Gentry in Hot Springs,

North Carolina, in 1916, he and Maud diligently collected her amazing repertoire of 'love songs' (as ballads were commonly called in the Appalachians) but completely missed her rattle-bag of Jack-Tales, which were simply not on their radar. It would take future collectors to acquire these.

Such blind spots within any specialist field are common, so it not surprising to see them occur in the folk music and storytelling scenes: folk festivals seldom book storytellers, and never give them prominent billing, however established they might be. Storytelling festivals are rarer and perhaps more keen to have the crowd-pulling power of established folk music acts; but storytelling clubs, although often open to musicians, generally don't encourage the democratic singarounds or 'sessions' that you get in folk circles. And the two audiences, demographically almost indistinguishable, seldom mix. Although both undeniably part of the oral tradition, they seem at times to exist in separate universes, albeit with notable exceptions (e.g. Hugh Lupton and Chris Wood; Daniel Mordern's troupe, The Devil's Violin; British-Bulgarian performing arts group, A Spell in Time; or Richard Selby and Beth Porter's collaborations in the Bath Folk Festival to name a few). This seems to me to be to their mutual impoverishment, because enthralling cross-fertilisation can occur, as I've experienced in the group I co-founded, Fire Springs, and more recently with my partner, Chantelle Smith, in our 'ballads and tales' duo, Brighid's Flame.

In truth, folk music and storytelling exist in a fertile continuum, which practitioners on both 'sides' revel in, and the forms are far more porous than less open-minded promoters, publishers or producers would have us believe. Those with vision, the artistic innovators and the bold programmers, are always challenging such arbitrary walls.

So, with such a locus of interest (in particular my research into 'supernatural ballads' of the Scottish Borders) I became interested in the possibilities of narrative treatments. Having written two collections of folk tales for The History Press' county-by-county series (Oxfordshire and Northamptonshire), and contributed to *The Anthology of English Folk Tales* (2016), I had already written a handful of 'ballad tales' – that is creating a folk tale out of an existing ballad. I knew I was not alone in this and I felt the form could be pushed further.

INTRODUCTION

While the Folk Tales series emphasises the orality and aurality of the text, pre-empting the tales as potential resources for future performances, here I wanted to explore the literary possibilities alongside the performative. My *Ballad Tales* would be free to experiment without any expectation or performance of authenticity. So I pitched my idea to the publisher and the rest is history (press), as they say.

I invited writers and musicians whom I thought would fit the anthology well. Although I reached out to practitioners across the country and across disciplines the process was no doubt skewed by my own predilection: those whose oral, literary or musical skills I know and admire; who I have had the pleasure to collaborate with or see in action. That the contributors are largely a result of such elective affinities is perhaps inevitable and I make no apologies for that, but hope that if future anthologies result I will cast a wider net and hope for an even healthier diversity of voices.

I asked for imaginative, lateral retellings in prose of traditional British ballads – now those last three terms can all be deconstructed until the cows come home, but that is not our focus here. Basically, I was looking for pre-twentieth-century anonymous ballads from the British Isles (not 'ballads' in their strictly poetical form, or as a pop song, but as robust tale-songs from *Judas*, the earliest known ballad dating from AD 1300, onwards). This undoubtedly narrowed our scope, but makes an anthology like this possible. Other iterations might focus on different countries or themes.

Yet this seemingly narrow remit almost immediately was subverted by the submissions. Australian-born Eric Maddern's rollicking telling of the wide-ranging ballad of the *Flying Cloud*, 'The Pirate's Lament, or A Wild and Reckless Life', is perhaps the greatest exception to this rule as it roams the Seven Seas (being found in versions from the Low Countries to Scotland, Newfoundland to Nova Scotia and across North America), rightly challenging the questionable, Colonialist notion of an exclusively 'British' ballad – for a ballad, by its very form, memorable, copyright-free and travel-proof, is a moveable feast.

With each singular submission my notion of a ballad tale was expanded. I deliberately kept the brief open-ended. I did not wish to be prescriptive or to influence the way the writers went with their material. They chose their ballad; they chose how to adapt it. Perhaps it was a controlled experiment on my part – to see what the contributors would come up with independently – but it paid off. There is a splendid array of ballad tales here, ranging from the more 'traditional' approach, where the balladeer has worked *with* the grain of the ballad; to the more 'experimental' approach, in which the genre, gender, moral compass or plot of the original is completely subverted. That is not to say that the innovation only happens chronologically (as though to claim: the greater the distance, time-wise, from the original setting, the more innovative it is) as daring and dramatic volte-face can happen in *any* aspect of a ballad tale – in the nuances of characterisation ('Tam Lin'; 'The Storm's Heart'), dialogue ('The Darkest Hours, The Darkest Seas'), use of dialect ('The Droll of Ann Tremellan'), or telling detail ('Mary and Billy'; 'Nine Witch Locks'), to list but a few.

A tale told well enough transcends time.

It is perhaps no surprise to note that a few of the ballad tales feature cross-dressing ('A Testament of Love'; 'Ain't No Sweet Man'; 'The Shop-Girl and the Carpenter'), not due to a wish to jump on any fleeting bandwagon, but due to the simple, regrettable fact it is hard to find traditional ballads in which the female protagonist has agency, can act rather than be acted upon, and enjoys equal status to the male characters. That each respective tale is distinctive in tone and setting shows how even with similar sources good writers can conjure something original. And in terms of gender politics, such concerns are very timely and unfortunately perennial as two of the oldest stories in this collection ('What Women Most Desire', from the fifteenth-century poem, 'The Wedding of Sir Gawain and Lady Ragnelle'; and 'The Dark Queen of Bamburgh', based upon 'Kemp Owyne') show.

The later tales in the collection ('A Mermaid in Aspic'; 'The Grand Gateway'; 'Shirt for a Shroud'; 'The Wind Shall Blow'; 'The Migrant Maid'; 'The Two Visitors') illustrate in daring ways how the form can be recast in a contemporary or even future setting while still retaining its core truth. Here be dragons and mermaids (and men) in many shapes and forms.

To say much more than that might undermine the pleasures that await you. Each balladeer has offered accompanying notes, but I suggest deferring that gratification until after reading their tale. The Child and Roud Indexes have been used to reference each ballad (e.g. 'Child 37/Roud 219'), which you will find in the accompanying notes at the end of each chapter. These indexes are available online.

Now, pour yourself a glass and pull up a chair. You are in the company of bards and the hearth-fire is lit. In the dance of the flames glimpse those who've remembered and collected before us; in the hiss and crack of logs, hear the voices of those whose songs we tell.

Kevan Manwaring,
Stroud, 2017

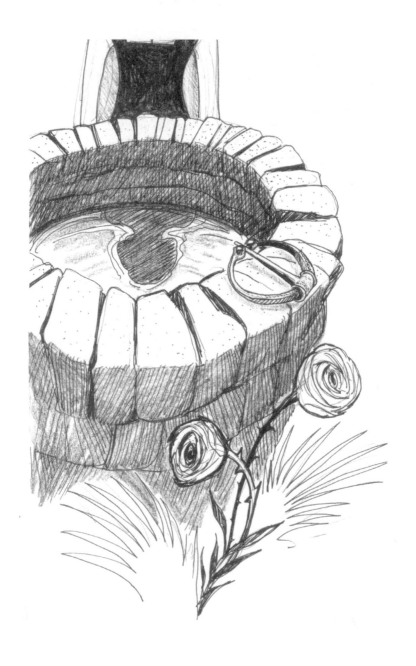

Janet and the Queen of Elfland

A Retelling of the Ballad 'Tam Lin' by Fiona Eadie

O I forbid ye, maidens a',
That wear gold on your hair,
To come or gae by Carterhaugh,
For young Tam Lin is there.

ANON, Scottish Borders

Long ago, in the borderlands between England and Scotland, there lived the Earl of March. His land covered moor and hillside, glen and trickling burn, but there was one place on his estate where people feared to go – and that was the well and the wood at Carterhaugh. Since ancient times it had been told that Carterhaugh lay within the fairy realm. The older people would say to the young, 'Do not go to that place, for if you do you will surely be spirited away and we will never see you again!' If any had to go by Carterhaugh, if there was no option, they would take a token – to placate the others – and leave it at the well.

Now the Earl had one bonny daughter, Janet. Strong, proud and feisty, she had reached an age where she was becoming restless and curious to know more of the world beyond her father's castle.

One morning in late summer, Janet sat looking out of the castle window, as the sun warmed the old stonewalls, the smell of heather floated on the breeze and the gentle hum of bees drifted in the air. In the distance, the blue haze of Carterhaugh woods beckoned.

'I will go there, I will,' Janet thought to herself. 'I will take a token and no harm will come to me.'

So she braided her hair about her head, she raised her kirtle above her knee and away she went. When she reached the well at Carterhaugh, Janet was enchanted. Soft grass grew all around, roses tumbled over the well and, beyond a small rounded green mound, hawthorn bushes shimmered in the sunlight.

Behind them the dark woods.

Janet took a brooch from her dress and laid it as a token on the rim of the well. Then she reached up and plucked a double rose, twined it into her braid and gazed down into the well to see how she looked.

As Janet straightened up, she felt a shadow fall across the water, blocking out the sun. An involuntary shiver became a shudder of alarm as she saw there on the other side of the well, glaring at her, a young man clothed all in green holding the reins of a white horse. The man's handsome face was stern, even angry, and when he spoke his voice was harsh: 'How dare you pluck that rose, lady, without my leave?'

'This wood is my father's; it is my very own! I do not need your leave, young man. And who are you, who haunts the well at Caterhaugh?'

'My name is Tam Lin. I am a knight from the court of the elfin queen. When you picked that rose, you summoned me.' They stared in fierce disdain at one another for a long time, both of them angry at the trespass and disturbance of the other. Then, unbidden, a force rose beneath that anger and something else was kindled between them.

Something strong and deep and sweet.

And so it was that Janet tarried at the well. And so it was that, as the summer afternoon progressed, they lay together – maid and knight – in the soft grass beside the well. And so it was that presently they slept.

When Janet awoke, Tam Lin had gone, a chill ran in the air and all the woods grew dim.

In the days and weeks that followed, Janet could think of little else except Tam Lin. Who was he? What was he? How could she see him again? She did want to see him again. Unwell and worried, she went to the oldest of her serving maids, who noticed her mistress's pallor and that her shape was subtly changing.

'I think my lady's loved too long and now she goes with child,' observed the maid.

Janet blushed.

'I know a herb, lady, grows in the wood at Carterhaugh, that would twine the babe from thee …'

So Janet braided up her hair about her head, she raised her kirtle above her knee and away she went. She passed the well, she reached the wood and, as she bent to pick a small grey herb, Tam Lin appeared.

'Oh, do not pick that herb, my love. Do not think to kill the babe that we got in our play!'

'Who are you, Tam Lin? What are you? Are you an elfin knight or are you a mortal man?'

Tam Lin replied, 'I was born a mortal man, grandson of the Earl of Roxburgh, and christened the same as you. One morning as I rode out by Carterhaugh, my horse stumbled and threw me onto yonder green mound where I lay senseless. The Queen of Elfland found me there and took me down into her realm to dwell, to be her knight.

'At first I liked it well enough, I was the queen's favoured knight and I had almost forgotten my life in this world but when you summoned me I returned and I remembered. After we lay together I knew that I want only to live once again in the mortal realm, to be with you … your husband and a father to our child.'

'Well then Tam Lin, what must be done to win you back?'

Tam Lin was silent then for a long while and when he spoke again it was in a voice of despair.

'There is only one way to win me back and that so fearful I do not know if I can ask it of you.'

'Tell me Tam Lin, what must I do?'

'Tomorrow night is Halloween, when the veil between this world and the fairy realm is stretched thin. On that night, as every year, the elfin court will ride. Every seven years they pay a tithe to hell and I fear that tomorrow – for all that the queen makes much of me – I will be that tithe. If you would win me back you must wait by the well at Miles Cross at midnight. You will see the elfin host pass by – first will come the queen herself and then two companies of knights. Then will ride by a black horse, then a brown horse and finally a white horse. I will be riding the white horse and you will know me because I will have one hand gloved and one hand bare. You must pull me down from my horse and hold me fast. When the queen sees what has happened her wrath will be terrible and she will change me in your arms into all manner of fearsome beasts. If you can but hold me fast, you will not be harmed. Finally, she will change me in your hands into a red-hot coal. Take this burning coal and throw it into the well and I will be returned, naked, to the mortal world. Cast your cloak over me and keep me safe until the elfin host has gone.'

The following night, an hour before midnight, Janet left the castle. Clouds scudded across the sky and the wind rustled among the trees. Although she had wrapped her thick cloak around her she was shivering, as much with fear as cold. As Janet stumbled towards Miles Cross, it seemed that every root tried to trip her and every branch snatched at her face. Forms and figures flitted by her, shapes and shadows stole around her. Finally, she reached the well and, as she hid in the bushes there, the clouds cleared and the full moon cast a cold light over the woods and the deserted road.

At first she thought they would not come but then, as midnight approached, she heard a sound that made her blood run cold. From far off along the road came the unearthly sound of fairy bells on harnesses and Janet saw a faint and eerie light as the host approached. First, came the Queen of Elfland herself, her long black hair streaming in the wind, her face proud, fierce – and totally other. Then two companies of knights and behind them a rider on a black horse, a rider on a brown and, finally, on a white mount, a rider with one hand gloved and one hand bare. Janet rushed out from her hiding place and pulled the rider down. She covered him with her cloak and, as both stood shaking in the road, the queen suddenly became aware of what had happened. She wheeled her horse around, pointed at the pair and gave a terrifying cry that rang out across the night: 'Oh, young Tam Lin's away, away! Oh, young Tam Lin's away!'

Suddenly, it was no longer a knight that Janet held in her arms. The queen had changed Tam Lin into a lion that roared and ripped and Janet thought her pounding heart would crack with fear. The rank smell of the beast, its strength and sharp claws threatened to overwhelm her but, somehow, she held on ... he was born a mortal man, he was born a mortal man she told herself over and over.

Then the queen changed him into a bear that clawed and crushed and Janet could feel its foul breath on her face. As terror flooded her whole being, she forced her quaking mind to focus on one thought: he was christened the same as me, he was christened the same as me.

The bear vanished and in its place a powerful and venomous snake twisted and twined in her hands. Paralysed with fear, muttering fiercely again and again he is the father of my child, Janet somehow held fast until finally the snake was gone and she was holding, instead, a red-hot coal. Beyond fear, beyond thought, Janet grasped the coal and she was not burned. She threw it into the well, there was a startling hiss and then, as she stared, a young man, naked, emerged from the water. She went to pull him out and once more threw her cloak around him.

At this the queen, in a voice of ice and fury, roared, 'Had I known you would be taken from me, I should have took out your eyes Tam Lin and put in two eyes of wood! I should have took out your heart Tam Lin and put in a heart of stone!'

Then with an angry, imperious gesture to her followers, the queen wheeled her horse around and led the elfin host away. As the eerie light grew dim and as the sound of fairy bells on harnesses faded into the night air there was left in the road, in the moonlight, only Janet and Tam Lin, their arms about each other, shaking but alive – a mortal woman and her mortal man.

I first came across the ballad of 'Tam Lin' (Child 39A) thirty years ago on a vinyl LP by Frankie Armstrong – won in a folk club raffle. I was captivated by it and by Frankie's voice and played that particular track over and over again until I knew the lyrics by heart. In the intervening years, I have heard many other versions but this is the one that has stayed with me and sits behind the Tam Lin story that I tell every Halloween.

❧ 2 ❧

The Tongue that Cannot Lie

A Retelling of the Ballad 'Thomas the Rhymer' by Kevan Manwaring

Syne they came on to a garden green,
And she pu'd an apple frae a tree:
'Take this for thy wages, True Thomas,
It will give the tongue that can never lie.'

ANON, Scottish Borders

May I be so bold as to sit by your fire? It is a dreich nicht and I am weary from the hard road. Thank you kindly, good sirs. I knew you to be gate-gangers like mysel'. Such times drive us onto the road, do they not? Ah, uisge beatha ... you are gentlemen! I've a lowin-drouth upon me. Slàinte mhath.

What's that, you dinnae ken Scots?

Then I shall do my best to speak the Sassenach tongue, although I would fain from calling it the King's English. Pisht. He may claim this whole land as his, but does Ironshanks own your words as well?

My tongue is my own! Some say I would do better at holding it. If I did I might not be in this spot o' bother. Well, there's no way around it now. I have the Tongue that Cannot Lie. And we live in an age where speaking the truth can get ye into a lot of bother. The powerful dinnae like their secrets being shared. And I have seen the spectral workings behind the world, the shadow games.

There I go again … anyhow, it was a gift, though I thought little of being given it at the time from a certain fine lady I know. And therein hangs a tale … To repay your kindness – a fire to dry my feet by and a flask to sloken this thirst of many hard miles – and to pass the dour-watch afore daybreak – let me relate to you my tale.

I was once simply Thomas of Ercildoune. Do ye ken it? Near Melrose Abbey, on the road to Edinburgh town. Easy enough to pass through without even noticing it. Like many a braw lad I spent my day in daydreams and tomfoolery, a-wondering what my destiny would be. How could I escape the mundane lot of my kind – to toil in the fields for some laird, tug on my furlock, cap in hand, whenever he passed on his fine horse, and be grateful for the thin gruel our kind are meted out while some dine in luxury off the back of our sweat? It had broken my father, turned him sour. Ready with his fists, living for his thirst. Made my mother immune to her misery, hidden away inside hersel'.

I would not let it break me.

I took to wandering the hills thereabouts – to the Eildon hills to the south. Three distinct peaks, said to have been split by the wizard Michael Scot. You know he summoned a demon to do his bidding, but then couldnae get shot of it, so he set it impossible tasks: tae split the Eildons thrice, and to weave rope from the sands of the Tweed – and the beastie is still doing it to this day. Like me spinning my yarn, which will ne'er end, I hear ye grumble, if I keep digressing!

So, there I was, mooning about the Eildons. 'Twas a glorious summer's day. You may not reck it now, on this foul Cailleach of a night, but Alba can be bonnie indeed. A break in the clouds and she's the most beautiful lassie you've ever seen. Which leads me to the start of my tale!

I was idling beneath a May tree, letting the sun and shade dapple my face, imagining the kisses of some lassie appreciative of my neglected achievements, soothing the bruises of my pride, when I heard a horse's hooves upon the lane, ringing bright and clear across the still hillside. I sat up and beheld a ferlie most comely.

Riding towards me was a queen – for her fine raiment and deportment suggested no less. She wore a dress the colour of rain-washed meadows, and rode a horse of the purest white. Its bridle glittered with silver, and from their jingling sound I fathomed they were bells. Their tinkling sent me into a kind of trance. Her fine, pale features were framed with a glory of coppery curls, which cascaded down her slender frame.

At first I thought she must be riding to meet some lord, but she turned her steed towards me. I quickly brushed myself down and bowed, low to the ground. I greeted her as the Queen of Heaven – flattery comes as easily to a poet as butter to a knife. We are born to praise the fairer sex. All that my father was *not* in his fist-talk, I *was* with my silk-words.

My lady declined such a high estimation of her rank. Perhaps she was as wise to smooth-tongue flatterers as I was to the wheedling of a cat looking for a saucer of milk. Instead, she revealed her rank and origin – which was even more astonishing. She was the Queen of Elphame, no less. You may find it hard to credit, but all I have experienced bears testimony to this truth, so I pray you to hear me out before you judge. Mind, I cannae tell a lie.

She told me she had come far from her homeland to visit me – yes even I found that hard to believe, but that was her purpose. For what reason? Well, who knows a woman's motives? Their actions are as fathomless as Loch Ness. Kittle kattle they surely can be.

She told me to join her, up upon her white steed, and to accompany her back to Elphame. Well, when a beautiful woman asks you to join them for a bit of a gallop, you do not walk away if you have red blood in your veins. At the time all I thought was: any excuse to get closer to that comely frame. And so without a second thought to my safety, my hearth and my kin, I mounted up behind her. Oh, to put my arms around that slender waist was almost more than a man could bear, and to smell the sweet perfume of that coppery mane. If that wasn't enough to put me into a swoon, then the jingling of her rein did the trick as she shook her bridle and off we set – and the bright Eildon hills became a blur as we passed beyond the Borders.

We wallopit down a green lane, which seemed to open up before us as we entered, the light and shade flickering by. I looked behind and the May tree I had sat by rapidly receded into the distance, a faint speck of light at the end of the elongating tunnel of green.

What's that? Oot o thocht, ye ken? All a bit far-fetched? By my guid dirk, I tell you it exactly as it happened. I can do no other. But if you found *that* hard to stomach, then you will not find palatable what is to follow. If it helps, then see it as a tale, a childish fancy to pass the dark hours. And, if truth be told, I can only understand it in that way – through the language of story. What I experienced ... no words can do justice to, but I will do my best to stitch together a patchwork of my impressions, a crude equivalent of the glorious tapestry that unfolded afore me ...

We rode on until it seemed the horse galloped across the night sky. A vast blackness engulfed us and an icy wind howled like the Cailleach's breath itself. And to my horror, my fair queen fith-fathed afore me – her comely frame became a thin sack of bones, her mane greasy straggles, her smooth skin sunk into her cheeks, and her fulsome breast drooped low to her belly. I held a skeletal hag, draped in black rags! She turned around and I was confronted by her hideous visage.

'Likes what you see, do you deary?' she cackled, blasting me with her foetid breath and making me gag at the blackened, toothless maw.

I recoiled, but looking down at the chasm around me I realised I had no choice but to cling on. What had I done? I would pay the price for my foolhardiness.

Oh, Thomas, for once, why did you not leave the lassies alone?

Onto the bony frame of the crone I had to cling for dear life, as we entered a drear wasteland, which seemed to stretch forever. The only sound now was a trembling boom and hiss, all the world like the roaring of the sea. I have beheld the white horses crashing upon the shingle, yet there was none here to see. All that I could bespy were burns gurgling with blood tumbling over the black rocks. My heart beat sore inside my chest, a drummer boy leading a doomed company to slaughter, and I trembled with fright, barely able to hold on. My limbs had turned to water. 'Come laddie, get a grip', I could imagine hearing my father saying, and for once I valued his stern admonishments. He would have the steel – had he not seen battle? He had the scars to prove it. If he could survive, so could I. Yet, I wondered, what dead lands did this hag lead me into?

We journeyed on in such fashion for what seemed like a whole moon's turning and more. The relentless rhythm – the horse's motion, the sea-music, the clomp of the hooves and the thud of my heart, made me fall into the stupor of a trance. Hours, days, weeks, passed, it seemed – though, in truth, time had no meaning there. There was no way to measure it – the sun and the moon remained hidden. The only light came from the stars, which glinted down like sinister eyes, and the dull red of the bloody cataracts beneath us. I thought I would expire through thirst, hunger or exhaustion, but the crone's strength was formidable and it was her will alone that kept us going.

Then, when I thought I could go no further, the horse stopped. It took some time before my body did the same – so used to its motion by then. We had broken our journey at the foot of a twisted tree – the sole vegetation in this bleak place. It grew naked upon a knowe except for a solitary fruit – the appearance of an apple, it seemed to suck in all the crimson of those streams, and was beaded with starlight. I was ravenous by then, and I leapt from the horse, stumbled, then scrambled up to the tree. I went to pull that fruit, but in a raven-winged whirl the crone was by my side, and her bony grip was on my arm. She bad me not to eat the fruit of this land. I would expire if I did not have sustenance, I pleaded. I fell to my knees, weeping.

To my surprise, the crone sat beside me and produced a meal from a knotted cloth – a loaf of bread, still warm as though freshly-baked, and a flask of dark wine. I looked at her, incredulous. She bade me eat and drink and I needed no further encouragement. My loathly companion did not join in this repast – I was too weak to be suspicious – but with each mouthful and draught a wonder occurred afore my eyes.

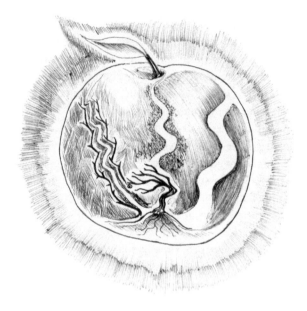

My strange companion grew younger and fairer until her former beauty was restored. I wept at her renewed appearance – whether this was her true sel', or the former, I did not care. This was fairer to look upon! The effect of the nourishment and her glad countenance made me weep with joy.

'The foul can be fair, Thomas, and the fair can be foul. It depends upon the heart of the one who sees.' Whether she spoke these words or no', they echoed in my noddle ne'er-the-less.

There was a break in the pall of clouds and moonlight illuminated the land – a vista, stretching out before us from that hillock like some map fashioned in silver and pewter.

I felt replenished for the first time in days – all the weariness of that long ride melted from me. My fair queen, once more in her glory, invited me to rest my head upon her knee, draped in the green again. With gratitude at her kindness, I did as she bid me. She stroked my hair and hummed a tune that soothed my cares away and stirred within me desirous thoughts. But she guided my gaze away from her beauty to the vision before us.

In the moon's light three glens were visible. With her long elegant finger she pointed to the first, a broad glen, which looked the easiest riding. 'That is the road to wickedness,' she warned, that voice again murmuring in my mind, 'though some call it the way to Heaven'. Then, she pointed to a narrow way, all tangled with thorns and briars. 'That is the road to righteousness,' she explained, 'though few that way travail'. Between these two extremes lay a middle way – a bonnie road. She said: 'That is the road to fair Elphame, and that is to be our wending'. But there was a condition. She placed a geas upon me, not to speak a single word – a hard condition for one so talkative as I, I'm sure you would agree. My father always said, 'Thomas, yer tongue gangs like a lamb's tail!' But bite my tongue I did – until now, when I can do nothing but speak the truth.

And so I will relate what befell us as we journeyed on – into —

Haud yer weesht! Do you hear it? I am sure I heard hounds? No? Forgive my fidgin; I have been pursued like a stag across the land since first I uttered my prophecies. True Thomas, they call me – for what I say comes to pass. But I get ahead of mysel'. First you must hear of my time in that other world. Seven years it was to be in the lawing, though to me it felt like only seven days. And as we have fewer hours than that afore the dawn, I'll keep it as brief as can be. One never knows when one's narrative is to be arrested, so to speak, so I find it best to cut to the chase.

Elphame. My words turn inside out when I try to speak of it. It is like this world, but more so. In comparison, this midden Earth is its sloughed skin. There, colours are more intense, sounds, tastes, sensations of every kind. The trees are more *tree*. The blooms, bonnier. The burns, clearer and cooler. Don't laugh. I'm not joshing with ye! You hav'nae seen birds like it – twice the size of the ones here. And their song, och! It made me weep to listen to the beauty of it.

My fair companion – still comely in seeming, at least – led me to her castle, sitting proud in its loch, the crown of the glen. We crossed the narrow bridge to the portcullis where we were greeted as returning royalty, which of course my lady was – sovereign of that realm. Blossom was festooned at our feet. A fanfare announced their majesty's return. A great banquet had been prepared. I was allowed to bathe after my long journey, and was given a set of splendid clothes to wear that fitted me to perfection. And then I was shown to the feast where I sat by my lady and enjoyed all that was presented to us – a meal fit for, well, a king. The entertainments were beyond compare. The wine, a waterfall. The guests beamed at us, saying we made a good match. It felt like a wedding, and in its way it was – for I was behoven to my lady for seven years, although I did not know it then. If I had known each day there was a year of my life gone forever from here, I would have felt differently about the whole thing. Instead, oblivious to the sands of time cascading away, I revelled in this elevated status, and in the sheer indulgence of it all, enjoying what I could only dream about as a mere son of a blacksmith from a humble Border town.

The next morning I woke up in a dungeon. The first thing I noticed was a rat inspecting my foot, deciding whether it was fair game or not. I kicked it away in disgust – it squealed and made a satisfying thud against the far wall, before scuttling drunkenly off. Groaning at my pounding head, I appraised my situation. Limbs bound in iron chains, check. A stinking straw-strewn cell with compulsory drip, check. Complimentary skeleton of long-term resident, check.

My fine garments were now my usual peasant rags – familiar in their threadbare comfort. The hangover seemed real enough though, whatever else had really happened the night before. Lord knows what they had put in the drink, but it gave me a blinding noddle. Which wasn't what I needed right then. 'Think, man, think', I told mysel' – hoping that my brain might start working at some point.

The comely lady, the long ride, the arrival – had any of it happened?

Then I heard a hacking cough. A half-digested rat was projected into the air, landing back at my feet. I turned my head with some effort and trepidation.

What I thought was a skeleton was in fact the hag, just finishing licking her lips, which were thin and black.

'Pardon me. I hate it when rodents repeat on you.'

'You! You brought me here. Witch, what devilry is this?'

The crone rattled her chains. 'Like my bells do you, deary?' She cackled. 'As you can see, Rhymer, I am as bound as you. They released me to summon a mortal male, but it was temporary liberty. While they hold my loved ones captive I had no choice but to obey.'

Was she telling the truth? From her situation she seemed to be. I let out a curse, which I shall not repeat here. 'Who are *they*?'

'The Usurpers. The Unseelie Court. Long have they coveted my throne. When my dear husband died – ruler of these lands for many a Great Year – the long-held peace was broken. They seized the castle, and threw me in here. I told them – do what you want to me, but do not harm my children. I *call* them that, but they are all grown up now. Yet still my bairns for all of that – big lummocks, but I love them. And they are all the more precious for being the last children born in this land. Somewhere in this retched place, they are kept alive – so I am told. I have to believe that.'

The hag wept, and I started to feel pity for her. Yet, she had lured me here, and anger swelled in my breast. 'Why? Why did you trick me here? To what foul ends?'

'Oh, don't jump to conclusions. The ends might not be as foul as you think.' She tried to shift her posture, tossing her lank locks over her bony shoulders. 'They want your seed, ironblood.'

'What?' I shifted nervously, making my manacles clink together.

'Elphame is barren. No child has been born here for centuries. Mine were the last. We are dying out, slowly, of extreme old age, of boredom. We love novelty. Play. Our empty nests pain us, and so we exchange mortal children for our changelings. And they provide some temporary amusement – but they soon become tedious when they reach that awkward age, you know to what I refer ... having not left it long yourself.'

Insolent hag, I thought, but I kept my tongue. The more intelligence I had the better my plan would be.

'We take them to our borders and abandon them. There I hear they wander, looking dissolute, seeking solace in sleep, mooning their days away – hoping to dream themselves back here. But we cannot be doing with their ... questionable body odour, mood swings, and vulgar behaviour. One day you will give this strange breed a name. I have heard it spoken of by our oracles – they will become a 'marketing category', whatever that means. Yaas, I think they're called. But for now, they exist betwixt and between – like us, caught halfway between man and angel, cursed by both, belonging to neither.'

I pondered the loathly lady's words. They were strange, but made some kind of sense. I remembered that feeling. Had I once been here before? Was that the reason it felt so familiar, like ... coming home?

'Mean the time, we wither and fade. Most of my kind look like me, but ... we like to keep up appearances. Make an effort, y'know? Today, though, I have let myself go. It takes it toll – sustaining the glamourye. But I'm sure you love me for my personality, don't you deary?' She gave me a blackened smile, and wiggled her cadaverous form at me.

Once more, I turned the air blue.

'Be flattered. They've brought you here to breed. Our men just don't have it in them any more. All gunpowder and no shot. They'll be a bevy of beauties like me,' she cackled to emphasize her point, 'queuing up for their night of amour. You lucky man! Think of them as milkmaids. Just lie back and do your duty for Queen and country.'

My mouth, dry as it was before, now felt like a desert – like the Holy Lands I had heard tales of. I strained to cross myself. A cold sweat broke out on my brow.

Then I heard an outer door clang open and heavy footsteps.

A brutish guard appeared, who carried a pail of water. Setting it down, he opened the cell and then carried it in. He had a face like a garderobe – slaikit mouth limed with his morning's repast.

'Morning, handsome,' my cell-mate hissed.

Ignoring her, the guard tossed the bucket of icy water over me. Gasping in shock, I spluttered more profanities, while he undid my chain from the wall and dragged me by it, out of the cell.

'Enjoy yourself, lover boy!' the hag mocked from the dark.

The guard clanged the bars back and, dripping and miserable, I was led up the stairs on my chain, a cur to its fate.

I was taken to a luxurious bedchamber, similar to the one in which I had first spent the night of the feast. Stripped naked, I was chained, spread-eagled, to the four posters of the bed. I strained against my manacles, but to no avail. They were of no metal I know – stronger than iron, yet lighter than copper. I called out until my voice was hoarse. The stone silence weighed upon me.

Then I heard the door click open.

I couldn't see who it was, half-hidden by the shadows and drapes around the bed. The light pad of naked feet made their way toward the bed. My heart beat in my chest and I licked my dry lips. To my horror, a bony, liver-spotted hand reached in and clawed at my flesh, long black nails gouging their Ogham marks.

I writhed, trying to wriggle free, but to no avail. I turned my head away but it was too late. She was before me, in all her foulness, and straddled me. Her bones strained against the parchment of her skin. A toothless grin salivated from between a witch-mane of grey. Each mole on her body had its own tuft of warts. A reek of rotting fish and seawrack defiled my nostrils, and then I was devoured.

I hope you're not uncomfortable with my tale, good sirs? I merely offer it to pass the small hours. Look, fair Aurora, she stirs in the east, and soon her bright cloak will banish the bad dreams of night, and I will be for the low road once again.

Hark, those hounds are closer now – each man's fate awaits him as sure as day must come. My tale must end, and I away.

She took me with a desperate hunger, crying out in pain like a beast whose wound only I could heal. But with each shuddering gasp a transformation took place – she grew younger and fairer, her hair a honey-coloured mane. With tears moistening her lips, she kissed me in grateful ecstasy.

She left before I could ask her name, but she breathed her thanks before departing, saying she would not forget.

Servants came in, bathed me there on the slouster bed. I was given fine food and strong wine to replenish myself with.

And then it happened all over again. And again. And as before, each crone became a woman in her prime, of all shapes, sizes, colours and persuasions.

The hours blurred into days. A week's toil. Were there eight of them or more? Hard to be certain in the sweat of it until, finally, it was done.

Exhausted, I was taken back to my cell, where I thought my time would be short – my purpose expired. My cellmate pried me with questions, asking for the particulars of this or that guest, whom she recognised from the tiniest detail. I sensed a certain jealousy in her interrogations. I was *her* Rhymer.

What was to befall us now? We awaited our fate in the dark. And there we got to know each other, sharing tales of our past.

In the darkness, her loathly appearance no longer mattered, and in truth, I had grown accustomed to aged flesh – isn't it the fate that awaits us all? I realised that behind every withered shell there is a soul who has lived a long and full life with all of its pleasures and pains. A soul who can still be beautiful beneath the ravages of time. For true beauty is the naked soul shining out of the cracked clay of our flawed vessels.

I had been broken open by every one of those women; touched by their simple, animal need for intimacy, for tenderness, for love. I had been granted a glimpse of their true self, beyond the glamourye, and realised that the bodies we wear are mere garments, garments that perhaps grow threadbare over time, an illusion that wears off.

Until we are free.

The queen wept at my words. She reached out and was able to touch me briefly with her fingertips. 'Thank you', she said. 'Rhymer, you have proved yourself a true bard.'

In silence we sat, awaiting our fate, but it was a different quality of silence – one of warm friendship.

The darkness was no longer so lonely.

The dungeon door was flung open and we shrunk back at the cutting light. We expected to be led to our execution. Down the stairs descended thin darkly robed figures, wielding torches. They lined up before our cell, faces hooded and beshadowed. I expected the worst.

But to my astonishment, they rattled the set of keys and opened the cell door. I recognised the bony hand in the flickering torchlight. It was one of the crones; and the others, I now recognised also, their bonnie bloom faded once more.

'Thomas the Rhymer, we release you.'

Before they could do so, I pulled back. 'No. Do not free me, unless you release the queen from her chains also.'

The dark sisters considered this. 'To have her bind us in chains?'

The queen finally spoke. 'No. Such bitterness is past. We are all changed by this ironblood bard. He has helped us remember our hearts. I forgive you, sisters. Let us rule this land together, in peace. In council we can govern. The time of men and wars is over.'

And so the crones released the queen too. Stiffly, she stood to her feet, refusing any help. She turned to me and took my hand. 'I shall not forget, either.'

Before I departed their realm – ruled over by the nine sisters now – I was given three gifts: boots of the elven sheen; a cloak of green, green cloth; and ... the Tongue that Cannot Lie. My boots and cloth you can see before you in the gathering light – they allow me to travel at great speed, and remain hidden when I need to. They have saved this Laland hide more than once. And the Tongue, gifted to me in the form of an apple from the queen's own orchard ... a shining fruit which blessed me with the gift of soothsaying ... a mixed blessing, for it gets me into bother as often as it gets me out of it.

Well, you have heard that for yourself to gauge.

But now I must bid you ae fond farewell. Thank you for your fire, good company, and fine uisge. The King's Men are on my tail. If they pass this way, then tell them a lie. You have not seen True Thomas. You have not heard his contraband words. Such clash that fades this side o' time.

I have been performing my version of this powerful, initiatory ballad ('Thomas the Rhymer/True Thomas' Child 37/Roud 219) since the early nineties, when I tweaked the words to fit my Sassenach mouth (to avoid delivering the Lowland Scots in a hammy accent). On the page, however, you can use dialect and the reader's imagination to do the work that only the best actors (or native speakers) can get away with. Inspired by Thomas's tale, I went on pilgrimage to the Eildon Hills as a young bard-in-training, and spent a windy night there. My tent nearly blew away (with me in it) but I didn't get to meet the Queen of Elphame. I've been back several times since, drawn by the Borders and the spell they weave with their ballads and tales. With my partner, Chantelle Smith, I have co-created a show based upon the tales of True Thomas (and Tam Lin), 'The Bonnie Road'. They seem to be part of the same mythic ecosystem, and I devised a workshop called the Wheel of Transformation, which explores their complimentary motifs. There is much to work with in both, which my PhD novel-project, The Knowing, *explores in detail. Each of us can have our own relationship with these ballads — and can return to them again and again to gain fresh insight. Here, I have had some fun, revelling in the dynamic between teller and listener, and the (possibly) unreliable narrator.*

❧ 3 ❧

Mary and Billy

A Retelling of the Ballad 'The Pretty Ploughboy' by David Phelps

It's of a brisk young ploughboy, he was ploughing on the plain,
And his horses stood down in yonder shade.
It was down in yonder grove, he went whistling to his plough,
And by chance there he met a pretty maid, pretty maid,
And by chance there he met a pretty maid.

ANON, England

In those days plough persons did not sit in nice warm tractor cabs listening to Radio 2 and eating Hobnobs while they worked. They had to keep a straight furrow using their own strength against the heavy wooden plough and the cussedness of horses. It was not a very nice job (but then, very few jobs on a farm were), but it was a skilled job and a man could take pride in his skill and his value to the community. Too often he had to plough in cold rain, with only some old sacking doing a poor job of keeping him dry, but sometimes the sun would be shining and he could take his shirt off and feel the warmth on his back.

Billy Mallon had been the sort of child that made the old ladies of the village coo over him. With a round sun-tanned face and long blonde hair, he became accustomed to receiving little titbits from them when they visited his mother. He grew up into a handsome, strapping lad, helped by the demands of his profession. Soon he became aware that he was turning the heads of the younger maids of the villages around. But this did not make him big-headed or cruel. His pleasure was to be good at his trade, ploughing, which his father had taught him. He loved the sweat tang of the horses, the feel of the red Herefordshire clay against the mouldboard of his iron-shod worm-turner. He was a calm man and horses felt safe with him.

He had to keep his mind on the task but he was also aware that Mary Wilton, the daughter of the farmer for whom he worked, was paying more attention to him than she should be. When he came to collect his team in the early morning, when farmers' daughters have every right to be still abed, she would be in the yard pretending to be carrying out some task. In the day he might catch some sight of her watching him from on top of the hill or hidden in the withies. At dusk, dead tired, he still had the strength to find his heart racing when he caught sight of her looking out of her window. Soon it got to the stage when he was looking out for her as much as she was looking out for him.

For Mary the early summer had never been so bright.

It was a hot late summer's day when she came to him, under the pretext of bringing him some bread and cheese and a small barrel of cider. He had been ploughing in the hay after the sheep had finished with it and his team and he were taking a breather under the shade of some trees. As she approached he was terribly conscious that he had his shirt off and he could suddenly feel every heavy breath of wind on his back. He blushed and he could see that she was blushing also, although her eyes were demurely downcast.

'I thought you might like some bait, to help you keep going.'

'Thank you.'

Their hands touched as she handed over the basket and their eyes met and both knew that no one else would do for them. She walked away quickly but both spent the rest of the day and that night thinking about the other and hoping the other was thinking of them.

So it continued for a while. Before long it was continuing in an altogether more serious state of affairs. There was nothing especially out of the ordinary for a farmer's daughter to bring sustenance to the ploughman, but a few folk were noticing that it was happening a little more often than was necessary.

Billy was a conscientious lad and he had the idea that his employer would not be too happy with the state of affairs. Old farmer Wilton was noted in the parish for his uncertain temper. 'Mary, my love,' he said one day, 'If your parents ever find out about us there'll be hell to pay.'

'Don't worry about them,' replied Mary, with the innocence of someone who had not seen much of the world. 'I'll just drop hints into the conversation about you and what a fine person you are. They'll come round.'

It was Mrs Wilton who first got wind of what was going on, from the idle chatter of the dairymaid. She kept an eye on her daughter and an ear to her dinner conversation, put the two together and came up with a much bigger number than she was happy with.

So she told her husband. He exploded. 'The blaggard! I'll set the press gang on him!'

Now, it was not as easy as we now think to get someone press-ganged. A sailing ship was the most complex piece of machinery then in existence and a captain had no wish to have someone on board who might pull the wrong rope during a tricky manoeuvre, especially if fighting the French at that particular moment, so press gangs tended to operate around sea ports. Also joining the navy was not the unpleasant prospect we think it. Life on board a ship was not markedly worse than for a poor person on shore. You could be pretty sure of regular meals and rum. In addition, there was the prospect of prize-money from captured ships. Many's the old sailor who funded a comfortable retirement thanks to a couple of hours of excitement.

Of course, you could also get your head knocked off by a cannon ball.

It was that last result that farmer Wilton was hoping for and, for a respected member of the locality, there were ways and means. The impress was a useful way for magistrates to get petty criminals out of the district. He went to see his friend and magistrate, William Myers, and informed him that he regretfully suspected his ploughman, a good worker but wayward, of poaching. Mr Myers took his role as magistrate seriously. He saw it as not so much upholding the law, but preventing any change in the status quo. He was more than happy to deal severely with anyone who threatened it.

Then it was easy to find a couple of toughs from Leominster who waylaid Billy on his way home and dragged him before the magistrate, together with a thoughtfully provided pheasant.

Old farmer Wilton congratulated himself on a job well done, but his horse-team never ploughed so well with any other ploughman. Even the earth seemed to miss Billy – the crops never grew so well after – and the farmer had earned the undying hatred of his daughter. A sensible girl might have put it all down to experience and go looking for the curate as a way of assuaging her sadness, but Mary was not sensible in that sense. She was sensible enough to dry her eyes and pretend that the world was going on much as it had before, although she felt as though it was coming to an end.

After a week of this and just as her parents were congratulating themselves for their good judgement, she went to her bedroom at the usual hour but, instead of getting into her nightgown, she dressed in her best travelling clothes. She waited until the house was quiet and then crept down, timing her footsteps to the steady beat of the grandfather clock at the foot of the stairs, to hide her steps on creaking floorboards, to the chest where her father kept his gold. With the help of her pocketknife it took only a moment to open it and she felt no compunction in putting every last sovereign into her reticule and then going out into the night in search of her jolly sailor bold.

Her plan was to set out for Portsmouth. She had heard it was a naval port and was sure that if she only could get there she would find Billy. But the world was bigger than she had thought and she was lonelier. A voice in her head told her everything was hopeless and the darkness around her seemed to be filled with every monster of her childhood.

She had set out walking but dawn having found her still within the fields she knew, she accepted a lift from a carter, who reliably informed her that her destination was many days away. In town she decided to invest some of her father's money in a coach ride, but there proved to be no direct routes to Portsmouth and she settled for one to Bath. She was pleased by how quickly it rattled along, taking no interest in the strange fields and new sights outside the coach window.

It was at a coaching inn in Bath, full of tobacco and the smell of strange beer and bodies, that her eyes fell on a young man wearing white canvas trousers, silver buckled shoes, a short jacket with large brass buttons and a checked shirt, all of which marked him out as a seaman. Before her courage failed her she went up to him and asked, 'Did you meet my pretty ploughboy, by name Billy Mallon, who has just been taken to the sea?'

He smiled at her with that special sailor smile and said, 'Pretty maid, will you ride?'

At this point the story can go one of two ways. Folk songs are full of sailors who show young women not what they were expecting and more than they bargained for. But this young man had been well brought up by his mother.

On the coach down to Portsmouth the sailor explained that, the fleet being quite numerous, he was not acquainted with this Billy Mallon personally. However, he did know that HMS *Weymouth*, under the command of Captain John Somerset, was taking men prior to leaving for the East Indies and any new recruits were very likely to end up there.

When the coach dropped them off at the harbour front at Portsmouth the sailor was able to point out the *Weymouth*, a fourth rate, standing off shore. Mary was horrified to see how far out to sea it was. How was she going to get to Billy? But the sailor smiled and said that her best bet was to seek out the captain and explain her predicament. Since captains tended not to spend all their time on the ship when it was in port they had a good chance of finding Captain Somerset in one of the many high-class establishments that senior officers tended to frequent.

Peering through the window of the third such establishment they came to, the sailor was able to point out the surprisingly young figure of John Somerset, sitting alone at a table and contemplating a large glass of wine.

'This is as far as I can go with you miss. Captains don't like being interrupted at their deliberations by common seamen ... but pretty young ladies are often another matter.'

Mary thanked him profusely for all his help, reached into her reticule and gave him five guineas for his trouble. The sailor thanked her with equal professions of gratitude and went to redistribute the money among the many taverns and young ladies of the town. He was not that well brought up, after all. Did he leave thinking she had any chance of success? He did not.

Mary might be quite innocent in the ways of the world but her mother had taught her enough about social niceties to know that farmers' daughters were not expected to talk to naval captains, especially when they were at dinner. But this was an emergency. Without taking time to think, she walked into the inn. The smells of roasting beef and thick gravy almost made her retch but determinedly she went over to the captain, who looked up, surprised.

'You have my pretty ploughboy, Billy Mallon, in your ship. He doesn't want to be there nor do I want him going off to the wars to be slain.'

She reached into her reticule and pulled out a great shower of golden guineas and dropped them on the table. Most denizens of the inn had already been watching her progress in shock but those few who had not now turned at the sound of so many coins.

'Here's a hundred bright guineas for you if you release him and, if that is not enough, I have twice as much more that you can have, only that you leave me the lad I adore.'

Now, again, the story could take several different turnings.

However, John Somerset *was* a honest man, not riddled with the greed that affected so many of His Majesty's officers, who preferred prize-money over protecting their country's interests, seeing war as a means of making money by other means. He was noted in the Service for the care of his men and had the lowest rate of desertion in the fleet. For a hundred guineas he could obtain quite a few experienced seamen at the cost of a man who could well be a liability. It was a bargain that could not be ignored. As he would when he was about to face a French frigate, he weighed up his options and decided that it was a bargain worth taking.

A message was sent to bring Billy ashore. While waiting, Captain Somerset engaged Mary in conversation and, after their discussion, was not afraid to voice the opinion that had he a shipload of Marys, resolute and bold, he would be a very successful commander indeed.

When Billy was brought in Mary threw her arms around his neck as she had often imagined but feared would never do again. Mary thought the bells of Portsmouth were ringing out for her and Billy. Cynics might note that the bell-ringers of the town normally practised at this time, but Mary knew better.

So they set off into the world to start a new life together.

Were they successful?

Well, they did have Billy's strength, Mary's resourcefulness and the matter of two hundred guineas in Mary's reticule. With that they had as good a chance as any.

And blessed be the day when all true lovers meet,
And their sorrows are all at an end.
This last cruel war called many lads away,
And their true lovers they never saw no more.

So sang John Morgan in October 1905, singing of a war one hundred years away, little knowing that, a decade later, an even more cruel war would call many lads away, to the heat of Gallipoli, the trenches of the Somme and the mud of Passchendaele. So we listen to it now, a hundred years later, not knowing what our own era holds. Every county has a version of this ballad, 'The Pretty Ploughboy'. Morgan's version, upon which this story is based, was noted down by R. Hughes Rowlands at the Pitch, Dilwyn, Herefordshire and included in Ella Mary Leather's The Folk-Lore of Herefordshire, *published seven years later, number 22 in her list of folk songs.*

The Storm's Heart

A Retelling of the Ballad 'The Grey Selkie of Sule Skerry' by Chantelle Smith

I am a man upon the land,
I am a silkie in the sea,
And when I'm far frae every strand,
My home it is in Sule Skerry.

ANON, Orkney

'Who the hell are you?'

'Please, put the knife down and I will explain.'

A flash of lightning illuminated the living room of the Rorbu cabin for a moment, revealing the man who had been hidden in the darkness. His eyes – eerily dark – were wide with alarm as he held out his hands in a gesture of harmlessness. The sight of him jogged a memory, the feeling that she should not be afraid of him, but life on her own had made the young woman cautious and she shook her head. Behind her the baby wailed in his cradle.

'No. You explain first. Who are you? What are you doing in my home?' Helga demanded, with more conviction than she felt. Her heart pounded, as it had done since unfamiliar fingers had brushed a lock of hair from her face while she slept and a soft voice had murmured to wake her. In the returned darkness, she could make out the darker shadow of the stranger and saw when he, at last, nodded.

'I am sorry. I did not mean to startle you,' he replied, his voice thick with an accent rarely heard in Lofoten. 'Do you truly not know who I am?'

Always in the wake of the storm.

Realisation hit Helga as though she had been punched. She breathed out sharply then waited for an explanation from the intruder.

'I went to the village first, but they told me you were no longer there. They told me about your child. Is he ... ?'

'Yours?' Helga lowered the knife. She looked at him hard. 'Yes.'

'I did not know.'

'Of course you didn't!' Helga snapped, bitterly. 'It is hardly something the village would broadcast far and wide – a daughter being thrown out because she was with child. They asked me who the father was and I could not even give them a name. For you gave me none.' Helga swallowed and shook her head, trying to banish the memory of her parents' faces as she had stood helplessly mute under the rain of questions.

'I am ... I am sorry. This is not a problem among my people; they would never have made you leave home for such as thing as this.' The man's voice was soft as he spoke. 'My name is Hein Mahler. Now you have that at least.'

'And you will take me with you, Hein Mahler, to these people of yours who will not see me as a disgrace?' Helga tried to keep the hope from her voice as she wrapped her tongue around the unusual name. She moved to a nearby, rickety table and laid the knife upon it before lighting an oil lamp. The room was at once lit with a warm, dim glow and she was able to see Hein Mahler properly at last.

He was as tall as the men of her village but where they were generally fair or brown haired, Hein Mahler's hair was smoky grey, although not from age. The thick waves framed a long, swarthy face dominated by a straight nose, thin lips above a short but strong chin and eyes that seemed darker than was possible. The rest of Hein Mahler's body was wrapped in a dark, oilskin cloak but Helga felt a burning within her as she remembered the body that had once pressed to her's in forbidden ecstasy.

'I do not think you would much like it.' Hein Mahler had been silent as she lit the lamp; now he spoke with sadness in his voice as

Helga hoped her cheeks had not betrayed her chain of thoughts. 'I live far from these Norwegian shores, on the island of Sule Skerry. My people are ... not as your people are.'

'You mean they wouldn't accept me, after all?' Helga could not keep the edge from her voice as her parents' words came back to her.

Spoiled. Unmarriageable. Shamed.

'No, no. Not at all.' Hein Mahler shook his head. 'Just ...' his brow furrowed as he searched for the words he needed and failed. 'Come with me.'

Hein Mahler stood and walked towards the door, pulling it wide and pausing on the threshold as he waited for Helga to follow him. Beyond the door, Helga could make out the short wooden platform, supported by the same stilts that held her old Rorbu cabin above the cold waters of the fjord. Behind her, the baby cried and Helga turned towards the sound.

'He will be fine for a short while,' Hein Mahler assured her from the dark.

Outside the cabin, the storm had calmed. Helga joined Hein Mahler as he looked down at the water where the waves lapped against the wooden posts below.

'Watch.' He pulled his cape up and turned, melting down into the shadows.

At first, Helga thought that he had fallen over the edge of the platform and she cried out with shock, but when the gibbous moon finally shook off its shroud of cloud cover, she saw before her not a man, but a huge seal.

Helga took a step back, unable to understand what had happened.

'Now do you see? I am no man, but a selkie.' The seal spoke with a man's voice even as his shiny black eyes looked up at her. 'Knowing that, would you marry me?'

'I do not see how that would be possible,' Helga managed to stutter around her tumbling thoughts and astonishment. 'Will this happen to our son as well?'

'Perhaps. The years will tell.'

Thunder rumbled in the distance and the waves swelled once more; the seal turned his head and looked out at the wide, dark waters.

'The storm will return again soon and I must go. Take care of our son. I shall return in seven years and we shall see whether the sea calls to him or not.'

Helga stared into the seal's unearthly eyes, fearful of the possibilities her lover had hinted at. A flash of lightning filled the sky and Helga's sight. When her vision cleared, there was no sign of the seal other than a circle of ripples in the dark water below.

Seven years passed.

Seven years of watching her son grow into a sturdy, fearless boy who could outswim any other child in the village. Seven years of teaching her son not to look others directly in the eye for fear they would see his whiteless eyes. Seven years of gaining a grudging acceptance from the village of her birth, and the parents who had disowned her, all due to the championship of Ramberg's headman, Leif, who had always loved Helga despite what others had thought. Helga had welcomed Leif's attentions and was fond of him although she did not love him. He was caring and kind, and in him she saw the possibility of stability and a place for her son in the eyes of her people.

Helga was halfway through packing a trunk with her meagre collection of clothes, smoothing down the flower-embroidered blue fabric of her best skirt and bodice, when she heard her son's frightened voice call from the room beyond.

'Mama?'

The hairs on the back of Helga's neck and arms stood on end as she turned, hurrying into the main living room, half expecting the sight that met her.

'Helga.'

'Hein Mahler.'

Outside, the wind howled and the rain was thrown against the red-painted wood of the Rorbu cabin with such violence they had to raise their voices to be heard. Helga took a deep breath as she looked upon the selkie who had returned as he had said he would.

'Haakon. Come here and meet your father.'

The little boy shuffled forward towards the figure who had intruded upon the peace of the leaking, creaking cabin.

Hein Mahler took a step forward and gently tilted the chin of the child so their eyes met. The selkie looked down at his son for several moments before nodding his head and moving his hand to pat Haakon's thatch of dark hair. He looked up at Helga and pulled a small, shining object from the depths of his slick cloak.

The ring gleamed in the lamplight.

'Marry me, Helga. Take this ring and come with me to Sule Skerry; you, me and our son, we—'

'I can't.' Helga's reply cut across whatever Hein Mahler had intended to say and she saw his shoulders slump in defeat. 'I am sorry.'

'Very well.' Hein Mahler looked back at his son. 'Then ... then at least let our son, Haakon, come with me. Give me his next seven years as you have had his first. After that he can decide where his future lies.'

'I don't know ...'

'Helga, the sea calls to him and I can see you know this as well as I. If he comes with me, I can at least teach him a greater knowledge of the sea than any fisherman knows. I can keep him safe. Please let me do this for my son.'

Helga fought down the urge to refuse Hein Mahler, instead turning to look at her young son who seemed, above all else, confused. She knew there was truth in the words of the selkie. If only the thought of being parted from him did not make her heart ache so much.

'Seven years, and then you will both return. Haakon alone gets to make his choice.' Helga smiled at her son, hoping he could not see the fear in her eyes, fear he would choose the world of his father above her own.

'Thank you.' Hein Mahler reached into another pocket and pulled out another, longer, golden object. 'Haakon, this is for you.'

He draped the finger-thick gold chain around the boy's neck and fastened the clasp.

'So your mother will know you, should we come to visit her.' He smiled down at his son. 'Now, say farewell to your mother and wait outside for me.'

Helga watched as Haakon fingered the gold chain around his neck before he dashed towards her. The boy wrapped his arms around her neck, burrowing his face into her neck. She felt the wetness of his tears against her skin, smelled the salt in his hair, and hugged him closer.

'It is good for you to go with your father, my Haakon. Seven years will pass quickly and I will be waiting for you when you come back.' She held him for a moment longer before gently disentangling herself from his arms. Helga kissed Haakon on the cheek and then watched as her child swallowed his remaining tears and solemnly left the room.

'You will look after him.' It was a statement, not a question.

'I give you my word,' Hein Mahler bowed towards her. 'There is something else I must tell you. A prophecy that brought me to you and our son. You must promise, Helga, *never* to marry a hunter. If you do so then your hunter-husband will go out one fine May morning and he will shoot me … and he will shoot our son.'

'What do you mean? Who said this?' Helga felt the colour drain from her face. 'Tell me. *Tell me!*'

'I cannot say more,' Hein Mahler gently pushed away Helga's hands as they grasped at his cloak and his arms in panic. 'I have already said too much. Please, trust my word on this. Remember the prophecy, heed it, and our son will be safe.'

The selkie moved so quickly from her that Helga had barely drawn breath to demand a further explanation when she found herself alone in the room. By the time she opened the door there was no trace of Hein Mahler or Haakon on the platform beyond. The wind and the rain struck Helga's face as she looked out onto the churning sea. The selkie's warning rang over and over in her mind even as she tried to convince herself that prophecies were godless things that prayer could protect against.

Helga chose not to heed the selkie's warning.

For six years she used every ounce of ingenuity and guile to ensure her husband, Leif, never had cause to be out hunting on a May morning. The spring of the seventh year brought the long-awaited melt to her homeland and Helga allowed herself to hope for the return of her son so that she could once more protect him from harm and so outwit the prophecy given to her on a storm-drenched night.

'My son, my son,' she called from the shore where she had gone on the first morning of May, telling her husband she wished to see the fishing boats leaving the fjord for the dangers of the sea.

Seals bobbed in the waves, one wearing a golden chain, but none of them showed any sign they knew her.

Had her son not been wearing the chain, she would not have known him from any other seal swimming the coast of Lofoten. 'Haakon, don't you know your own mother, my son?'

Helga's heart fell as the seal with the chain slipped below the waves and she left, wondering if her son had chosen to forget her and embrace the world of his father.

When the sickness fell upon her that evening, it was sudden and the fever burned through her so that she hung between the world of the living and the world of the dead, oblivious to all that was happening around her.

'Helga?' Leif's voice came to her through the darkness.

Helga opened her eyes a fraction against the light from the lamps burning in the small room. She saw Leif's face looking down at her and heard voices from the edges of the room praising God for her recovery.

'How long?' she asked through parched lips that cracked and bled as she spoke.

'Three days. We thought ... we thought ...' Leif's words faded to a hum as Helga's fingers closed around a thick, cool length of metal that had been wrapped around her fingers. She angled her head so she could see it better.

It gleamed gold.

'What is this?' Helga felt her body begin to shake with fear even as she silently prayed she was wrong.

'Well, it is a rather strange tale. I was unable to sleep yesterday morning after the doctor had sent me away from your bedside so I went for a walk along the beach, and what should I find there but two seals and one with a bright gold chain around its neck.'

'So you killed them!' Helga cut across Leif's explanation, unable to contain hysterical laughter that spilled from her as she realised what had happened. 'Of course you did.'

'I don't understand ...' Leif's expression fell as Helga turned her face away and her laughter became sobs. 'Helga. Helga, please, what is it?'

'Get away from me, Leif, get away!' As she pushed her husband's hands away, the horror and the grief overwhelmed her and a raw scream ripped its way from deep within her. She closed her eyes, knotting her blanket within her fists, not knowing if she would ever stop.

When Helga left the village of her birth weeks later, following the sandy beach that curved between the fjord's waters and the great mountains that dwarfed all else, she did not see the two figures watching her from Leiholmen in the middle of the fjord.

'Why can't we tell her? This isn't fair. It has broken her heart.'

Hein Mahler looked down at his son, sadness naked upon his face.

'The prophecy was for her. If your mother knows you are alive then you will still be in danger. Now she thinks you are dead, then you are safe.'

'But you tricked her. We tricked her.'

'Yes, but there was no other way once she had married the hunter and that she chose for herself.'

The uncomfortable silence between father and son was only filled by the cries of seabirds swooping from the cliffs and the sloshing of waves against the base of the island from which they watched. Hein Mahler sighed and shuffled to the edge of the rocks.

'Come, my son. There is no more to be done. Let's return home.' The selkie dove into the waters and out of sight.

Haakon stayed for a while, watching the figure of his mother become smaller and smaller until she was completely lost from sight.

'Goodbye, Mother. I love you. I will tell our story, I promise.'

Haakon blinked his dark eyes then turned his back upon the land of his birth and slipped into the cold, dark water of the fjord.

'The Grey Selkie of Sule Skerry' (Child 113/Roud 197) is a fantastical ballad I love singing unaccompanied, save for my shruti box. Unlike many versions of the selkie myth, this ballad features a male selkie, which makes it unusual.

I've always felt that the ballad portrays the mother as being rather passive so I wanted to make her more assertive and trying to make the best of a bad situation, even if thinking she could outwit the prophecy doesn't end well.

❦ 5 ❦

The Darkest Hours,
The Deepest Seas

A Retelling of the Ballad 'The Demon Lover'
by Richard Selby

The young man he was prest to sea,
And forc d was to go;
His sweet-heart she must stay behind,
Whether she would or no.

ANON, Scotland

He had cut the scraps of mutton, the vegetables and added liquid
from the pot. Then placing it on the tripod, banking the wood below,
he gave a stir. He knew he could walk the three miles, there and back,
and be sure the food would not spoil. He made his mother comfortable. She would stand and turn the pot once. He pulled on his hat,
wrapped a scarf round his collar and set out into the ever-blowing
spring wind.

He was a grafter; he could turn his hand to anything. He'd built
boats with his father, the wooden cottage they lived in, his sister's
cottage too. But with fewer boats and hard times there was less building. He would fish, he would harvest, he would raise sheep and goats
(the vegetation of the Ness was too harsh to keep a cow).

He made for Holm Stone. He walked there in all weathers. The rough holly circle drew him like a magnet, but at this time of year and this spring in particular, there was something else.

Earlier years called them Egyptians, but now Roma, travellers originally from distant lands. He knew they were here to work from spring through to autumn: harvesting grain in the uplands, soft fruits, apples, then hops. He knew where they were; they had camped there in other years.

They stopped work to stare at him, but as he had become familiar they took less notice. Some even acknowledged him and there was one who would look and he would look for her. She might carry something across the camp. She would stand, her eyes bright, observant and enquiring, sometimes even smiling.

It was late afternoon, a tune drifted with the wind and gulls towards him. A swerving, compelling song, reeling all in. Some tentative swaying as the people started their evening chores. He stopped to listen and there she was at the back of the camp. He walked on a few paces and there again, much closer, how quickly she moved! This time she talked: 'You're here again mister. I've seen you this way before.'

'Well I live nearby, other side of the Ness.'

'You like to walk over here? To see what you see?'

'I walk here to enjoy the space, sky, sea and now to hear some music.'

'Anything else?'

He smiled.

They both smiled.

And so it began.

The conversations became frequent on his evening walks. He found his steps hurrying across the shingle. She was friendly; though not always, for there were days when she changed, challenged. When there was a different light in her eye. Though mostly it was sunny. The warmth of her smile, words and then the touch of her hands, a brush of her arm. He was lost.

One evening a different mood, an unexpected appearance. He had seen her far off and then she was beside him. Hadn't she done that before?

'I move fast, our people have to,' was her explanation. A smile and a toss of her hair.

'I always thought 'Gyptians would have a different voice, more of another land, but you seem … natural.'

'My family have come here three generations. Women find it easier to blend, dealing with town folk. We spend a six-month here, six-month in the west. We try and ease in. Not so the men, they won't change their tongue, but it's the women who trade, so … and … we're not 'Gyptians, not Gypsies. We're Roma, proud of it!'

'Sorry, I didn't mean harm. I'm curious, 'tis all.'

'Curious is good. I can like curiosity.'

In coming days, he would be welcomed by the fire, cautiously, never by all. He watched as the people danced and sang their way through the night air, the music re-asserting their independence, soothing their savagery.

The two grew ever closer and though there was much opposition a formal betrothal was arranged, then a marriage planned. The air had rung with arguments but the two would not be denied. The day came, at the simple wooden chapel on the Ness. Then at the encampment when both families celebrated long into the night.

A calmness came and living was good. There was a new black-boarded cottage on the Ness and happiness flowed with the tide.

It could not last.

Times were troubled; there was talk of war sweeping through the land. Work was hard to find. Few were building, few could buy the fish that were caught and poor weather brought little to the land. Hard times brought hard decisions. The port had to supply ship and crew as decreed by ancient charter. The enlisting had begun in the port and his reasoning was that if he volunteered then there was some advance money and his service would have an agreed span. If he waited for the press gangs, his service would be harder and longer. Again the night air rang with words, not arguments but pleas and persuasions, for there was a child due in the spring. Go now he said and if all went well he could be back early in the year, in time for the birth. He knew he must take the seaward path. The offer of advance pay was only for two days.

So, the next day they walked together along the strand, shingle banks giving way to dunes, the inward tide on their right and within far too short a time they were at the port, hugging and bidding wordless farewells; tears bedecked her eyes and the ship was pulling out into the Channel and sailing to war.

Time passed, slowly at first, then, the business of providing for winter was upon them: wood to be gathered, weaving wool from the few sheep they had, this to be sold at market. News came sometimes and then the New Year: bitter cold from the driving winds off the Channel. She looked constantly at the barren landscape. There were small daily tasks that grew as she grew with the new life inside her.

One day news came, agonising news: a loss at sea that snatched at the hearts of the community, brought worry, then hope. The port's ship had foundered off the Spanish coast; not all had survived. There was confusion in the story that came home: a wild storm, two small boats making away from the sinking ship, one reaching land but the other breaking on the rocks. Some from that boat were saved, but who and how many? After many slow days names reached home, and their owners were not long behind. For her, no news, no certainty. She struggled to the port twice a week, scanning the lists of mortalities and of the living, but the name, the words she had learned to recognise, was not there.

A desolate time followed. Soon enough it was her time and in early spring on a clearing day, one year from their marriage, the child was born. A small but sturdy girl with eyes full of wonder for the seer and the seen. A perfect child. A child with a depth in her eyes. A child that grew with her mother's care and love. Summer brought the rest of the child's Roma family as they returned for harvest work, what little of it there would be. But for now the loss of the child's father clouded the dawning summer and any brightness it could bring.

Another summer had passed. Winter was approaching again, nearly two years since he had set sail. The child was growing. There was companionship with her husband's sister and her two daughters. The children often sat and played and gurgled together at the sister's cottage; the girl favoured solitude these days.

These past few months there had been an occasional visitor, dark-eyed and tall. He had appeared at dusk once: 'Madame, forgive me for asking ... but the day is powerful hot and I wonder if I might ask for a portion of ... some water.'

'Of course sir ... water ... a portion for a traveller. I've been a traveller. I'll fetch you some.' She returned with a cup from their supply.

He spoke: 'You live here with your family?'

'With my child, my ... husband ... he went to sea. He never returned though. I still hope ... maybe someday I'll hear his steps along the shore.'

'Well that's sad.'

'But have we met before? Somewhere. Not here. You I recognise.'

'Some would say all of us have met before. Do you believe that? There are other lives we have lived and perhaps that's true – a shared past?'

'Other lives?'

'Yes, other. I'll explain another time.'

'In another life?' She smiled. There was a small shift.

The passings continued, often at dusk, the request for a portion of water.

Some folk spoke straight out. He's been here before. Not to be trusted. But they continued and those visits often coincided with her being alone, the sister having taken the children across the marshes for a day.

It had begun.

Words, smiles, thoughts and little deeds as the stranger slid into the mother's life, perfectly finding the moment of loneliness and helping it pass. Smiling at those who mattered, though only half-smiles came back. When the child's aunt suggested a few days with another cousin across the other side of the marsh, there was no thought or worry. Grandmother was up to travelling in the cousin's cart. What could be nicer? They would look after the child. The mother had wanted to rearrange the small cottage, replace some items, make curtains from off-cuts that had come her way. The tall, dark-eyed gentleman was to be away so there was no nuisance from him.

Within hours of the departure, there he was.

'It's you ... I hadn't thought to see you here so soon.'

'Well my business away was nothing and I had to return. I thought I would call – for a portion?'

'You and your portion!'

'You seem to be ... alone. Your child away?'

'I'm alright thank you and there's those I can call to if I need. Don't worry about me.'

'Pardon, I shouldn't intrude, but ... tomorrow I must go to the port. You could come with me; there is something I would like to show you. We could go at first light. I need to pass this way. You might think of this?'

'The port? Why would I want to go there? And first light ... might seem I'm sneaking out.'

'It's just a short outing.'

'Well ... I haven't been there for some time. Perhaps.'

'I shall pass here early – I'll call. First light.'

'I'm not saying I will but not that I won't.'

How and why she found herself at the port, she wondered? The meal that they took in the inn was delightful; a glass of wine would do no harm and was this fine ship really his? He said there were more. Was he that wealthy? He paid for the meal from a full purse. And why should she not have this simple dress he offered her? The day moved so naturally. The notion of the short voyage to see his other ships at anchor was harmless. She was greeted by the man at the top of the gangway.

'Madame, it is an honour for this fine footstep to grace our vessel. Sorry for these sluggardly men. Jump you useless buggers! Move for the lady! Sailors, listen to 'em grumble. "Best sailors never wailers." That's what they say. If these matelots complain I treat them with a healthy portion of extra work and fewer rations. That'll keep them happy, then I'm happy too. The ship goes and we all go. Just so!'

'I think so, yes.' She was bemused by this broadside of information.

'So! You join us to sail. My master is proud; he would show not just this vessel but others. He has others.'

'Yes, he said.'

The master ordered cast off, reassured her she would be home before nightfall. A few hours passage would impress her, then, back to the port.

What could be nicer?

They transferred to a finer ship. Was this his? It looked so ... so grand. Already there was the feeling in her that had been long suppressed. A yearning for open ways, for adventure. Now, as she stood on the deck, the sea reaching out beyond, there were new beginnings. Shadowy figures let slip the sails and the ship began to move. She stood near the prow and looked out.

One small shadow slipped across her mind as she thought of the child, but she would be soon back. Perhaps more time could be spared, not just the two hours he spoke of. Surely it could bring no harm? Perhaps he would call a carriage to take her home if night had already fallen.

No harm.

'No harm at all! Trust me.' He had silently moved in beside her. Was he reading her thoughts?

She smiled nervously but then turned again seaward and the ship ploughed into the great Channel – prow to the waves, stern to the land and all other thoughts were left in their wake.

Somehow the hours turn to days, the days gather and they are sailing in the far Mediterranean. There is a change, calling at exotic ports where people talk in strange tongues but with words she recognises and music she knows.

It is the ninth day from the pass into the southern seas. It should be calmer but each day the sea rises. For now she can manage the pitching deck but surely it must calm soon.

She looks over the bows at the waves licking the flanks of the ship. Misting her and the deck and, always, the ninth wave the strongest.

She thinks back to the start of the voyage. To the first time he called for a portion of water. Had she always known him? Another time? Another life? Now he's here again.

'You're not to worry. Let nature take its course.'

'But I don't know my nature!'

'Then listen to me.'

His words enchant her. Her resolve slips. She looks across the seas. Far away there is a shore. A child. And ... someone missing.

The voyage changes. She can hear his voice, soft words and something else rises through her, creeps across her soul and now she looks into his eyes. His eyes,

which swirl like the sea, darken and change. Her soul changes. She opens her mouth. A gasp. She looks back to his eyes. All is lost. Then to the deck, to his leg, to his foot. The long elegant leg is now coarse hair, tangled. His elegant shoe is no more. A cloven foot and him now towering above her. His eyes purple. His forehead rippling change. She is lost.

The ship dives down the tallest wave yet. The ninth wave and its speed carries them down. Down. The air stills and there is a calm about them. A calm she does not feel for everything changes. There is a brief vision: a man and a child on a beach, a figure approaching, then it is lost. There are fish swimming in the clouds. The light stains and everything has a far-off feel. She is lost.

Back to the coast in the far south-east corner of England, the sister sits with her daughters and the girl with depth in her eyes.

Along the beach, shimmering in the heat haze, there is a figure, one who knows the land well, but he has been gone a long time. Lost they said, but after years of wandering he has returned. He listens to his sister, to the story, the story of his wife's solitude and how she went away. No one knew to where or why. Somehow he knew there would be this.

He listened with head bowed. Then he stooped and gently lifted his child. She looked deep into his eyes and he saw the past and the echoes and he held her and slowly she smiled.

Time slips again and the child was always with her father, playing happily. Then one bright day along the beach came a figure, shimmering in the heat haze. He knew the shape, his heart pounded as she approached and came to him and stopped ... but it was not her.

She was ... similar. The eyes were somehow different yet the same, he started to speak but she was there first.

'No it's not her ... it's another ... there were always two of us ... it was a game we played with you. I remember in the early days you nearly caught us so then we were careful. Then it was just her and the family ... sent me away.'

He remembered how sometimes in their early days she had never quite looked at him. He understood.

She talked a little, smiled and held the child but then it was time for her to go: 'I won't pass this way again. I'm away, back to the west.'

And she was gone – no talk of the missing – no expectation.

So he sits when he can, on the shingle beach, piling up the little stone cairn for the child to knock down and to laugh. He looks down, she looks up with rich deep eyes, they flicker. He looks out to sea to the cloudbanks that give the illusion of two mountain ranges, one dark with black heavy peaks, the other white with a clear shaft of light.

A peace settles on him and he looks back to the child's eyes.

'The Demon Lover' (Child 243/Roud 14) is just one of many titles for a ballad that stretches back hundreds of years. The ballad tells the story of a courtship by a tall dark devilish gentleman, as subtle and smooth a suitor as could ever be imagined. Things don't end well. This telling links the story to the Roma people who would take seasonal work bringing in the crops for the farmers of Kent. The setting is the Dungeness foreland that juts out into the English Channel and includes the enigmatic Holm Stone, a circle of ancient hollies. My family have had connections with this area for the last hundred years. Together with the musician Bethany Porter we have performed a version of this tale at Bath Literature Festival and Bath Folk Festival.

6

Nine Witch Locks

A Retelling of the Ballad 'Willie's Lady'
by Pete Castle

Willie has taen him oer the fame,
He's woo'd a wife and brought her hame.
He's woo'd her for her yellow hair,
But his mother wrought her mickle care.
And mickle dolour gard her dree,
For lighter she can never be.

ANON

Willie was his mother's youngest son, his mother's only surviving son, and so he was the apple of her eye and was indulged by her in everything he wanted to do. His mother thought no baby had ever been so beautiful or as forward as little Willie. He was perfect and unable to do any wrong, as far as she was concerned.

Willie and his mother lived in the castle that had once belonged to her husband, Willie's father, who had disappeared in mysterious circumstances not long before Willie was born. No one spoke about this except in whispers.

Who has killed the Master Kid?

The ancient castle seemed to grow out of a rocky outcrop and gave the impression of being as old as the ground on which it stood. It was perched on a high cliff overlooking a tiny harbour on a small, rugged island. A limitless sky stretched overhead – more often grey and filled with clouds and raging winds than blue with warming sunshine – and all around stretched a wild and dangerous sea, filled with reefs and islets. To the west empty ocean stretched to the horizon and to the south and east could be seen other islands of varying sizes from island to islet to uninhabitable rock. The people of Willie's island traded, fought, intermarried and squabbled with the people of these other islands and had done so for as long as anyone could remember. The mainland was remote and out of reach of all but the hardiest sailors and there were tales of other lands beyond that, but few had ever ventured there.

Right from the very beginning, rather than being a spoiled 'mother's boy', Willie was independent and adventurous. As soon as he could shuffle across the floor on his belly or his bottom he was into every nook and cranny of his mother's room. No cupboard was safe and any box or basket left at a reachable height would be turned upside down and inside out.

When he began to toddle no door could be left open or he would disappear and servants had to be dispatched to find him and bring him back. Sometimes it took them hours and he would be found in the most unexpected of places. Then the servants were terrified and tried to make sure it wasn't them who had the task of taking the baby back to his mother. All the common folk seemed wary of Willie's mother.

Who took out the combs of care?

By the time Willie was six or seven years old he knew every inch of the castle, from the deepest dungeons to the battlements of the highest tower. He was at home in all the back passageways and hidden staircases, the little niches and alcoves in which he could hide. He had managed to open all the secret doors and private rooms so that he could move around the whole castle without anyone knowing.

And he did not stop at the castle.

Willie's wanderings took him down into the town where he befriended the street people and tradesmen. He would be in and out of their shops, talking to them and helping himself to fruit or biscuits. His favourite place, though, was the harbour, where there was always the bustle of ships coming and going. He loved to watch the exotic goods being unloaded and would be entranced by the tales the sailors told when he asked about them – what they were and the strange lands they had come from.

The stories were so enticing that Willie decided he had to go and see some of these foreign lands for himself. For weeks he pestered and pleaded but none of the ships' captains would allow him on board so, one day, he sneaked up a gangplank and hid on the deck of a ship that was preparing to leave. That first voyage only lasted a few minutes as Willie was discovered before the ship reached the open sea and he was returned to the quay and hustled ashore as quickly as possible. Willie was puzzled by the way seamen behaved when they realised who their stowaway was. They went white and kept glancing up at the castle and trying to stay out of sight. Willie knew that his mother was not a woman to be trifled with but the townsfolk and servants had made sure that the rumours about her had not reached his ears.

Who has loosed her left-foot shoe?

All sailors are superstitious and none of those from that island wanted to upset Willie's mother and risk her casting a spell to sink their ship and drown them. They did not want to disappear in the way that Willie's father had disappeared. Willie in his innocence and youth did not understand this. His mother could be stern but he loved her.

But Willie also loved the smell of the sea and the movement of a ship and it made him determined to try to set sail again as soon as possible.

His second trip was not much longer but he did it with permission. A visiting captain, who did not know the boy and had not heard the rumours about his mother, agreed to take him round the headland to the next little port and back again the same day. Willie loved it but, knowing he would be in trouble when his mother found out, he made sure to take her back a present.

Magic tree ... go to sea ... go to see ...

For the next few years that became the pattern for Willie's adventures. He took longer and longer voyages – round the island, to neighbouring islands, and sometimes to the mainland, and he was away for longer and longer periods of time; but he always made sure to take his mother back a gift – a trinket or sweetmeat, something exotic and strange which she hadn't seen before. She pretended to be cross but could not keep it up for very long and Willie knew she would forgive him almost anything.

Left-foot shoe, tangled locks, singing in his head, underneath the lady's bed ...

As he got older Willie stayed away for days, then weeks, then months. He grew into a skilled sailor and began to know the world as well as he had known the castle when he was younger. He became a man: tall, tanned, muscular and fearless. He explored new lands, fought battles with the sea and with pirates, wooed young women in foreign ports and sometimes escaped from their fathers by the skin of his teeth. But he always returned home to be welcomed by his mother and he never forgot to take her an exotic present.

And then Willie went on a voyage that lasted longer than any before it. It began to look as though he would never return. The townsfolk began to whisper about his disappearance and compare it with the way his father had disappeared. Although she kept her thoughts to herself even Willie's mother began to fear the worse.

At last, after a period of many years, Willie arrived home. But this time what he brought with him was not a gift for his mother but a bride for himself – the Lady Regat. He had fallen in love with her long yellow hair in some distant land, had wooed her and married her, and now she was carrying his baby.

Nine witch knots ... nine witch knots ... locks of hair hanging there ...

It was not a happy homecoming.

Willie's mother was overcome with jealousy and wanted to keep her son for herself. Willie could not see this. He thought her initial reserve would thaw and she would come to love his lady as much as he did. Willie's wife knew that she was not welcome but, like Willie, she thought things would get better.

The weeks and months passed and the time for her confinement drew near, but there were none of the usual signs of a mother preparing to give birth. The couple checked and double-checked dates; they read the runes; they used old divination rituals; they consulted wise women and midwives. At first they consoled the anxious mother and assured her that everything was alright. She must be patient. They said that the baby would come when the time was right. It was not to be rushed, but they gave her potions to drink and watched the stars and the moon.

Nine witch knots ... the magic tree ... never, never lighter be ...

As the days passed Willie's lady told her husband her fears. She said that his mother hated her and wanted her dead. Above all she did not want the baby to be born so she had bewitched her. Willie told her not to be so silly; she was imagining it, he said. But she replied that she would never be able to give birth – never be lighter – until his mother allowed it.

More time passed and still there was no sign of a birth. Everyone was growing anxious. Then Regat persuaded Willie to go to his mother and take her a gift, from one woman to another. This gift was something she had brought from her home, something she valued highly. It was a beautifully carved and gilded cup of great value as an artefact, but it was of even greater sentimental value to Willie's lady as a family heirloom.

At length Willie delivered the gift and was astonished at the reaction of his mother when he presented it to her. She let out a cackle of foul laughter and flung the cup into a corner where it smashed amongst the dust and cobwebs. Then she shouted into Willie's face:

'Of her babe she'll ne'er be lighter, nor in her bower burn the brighter,
but she will die and turn to clay, and you will marry another may!'

Shocked and silent, Willie returned home and told Regat an expurgated version of what had happened.

A few days later she sent Willie to his mother again, this time with a message. She said:

'Tell your mother this:

Willie's lady has a gown, its like ne'er seen in all the town,
The gown is made of silken thread and stitched around with gold so red.
She will give this unto thee if you will let her lighter be.'

Willie went to his mother and delivered the message.

Again she stamped her foot, screwed up her face with hatred and screamed:

'Of her babe she'll ne'er be lighter, nor in her bower burn the brighter,
but she will die and turn to clay, and you will marry another may!'

Willie went back to his wife and admitted that she might be right. Perhaps the rumours he'd been gradually putting together might be right too. Perhaps his mother really was a witch and perhaps she had been responsible for his father's disappearance. Perhaps it explained various other strange things that had puzzled him throughout his childhood and youth too ...

Master kid, lady's bed, magic key, lighter be ... never, never burn the brighter ...

A few days later Willie returned to his mother with another message from his wife:

'Willie's Lady has a steed, its like ne'er seen in all the fells,
On its feet are golden shoes and on its bridle silver bells,
She will give this unto thee if you will let her lighter be.'

The reply was the same as before:

'Of her babe she'll ne'er be lighter, nor in her bower burn the brighter,
But she will die and turn to clay, and you will marry another may!'

Willie fled from her hatred.

By this time things were becoming serious. The baby was well overdue and Regat was becoming ill. She was wracked with pain and running a fever. Her belly was bursting and her limbs ached. She could not eat or drink or sleep. They consulted every midwife, wise woman, magician, sage who was willing to see them, risking the wrath of his mother, and they all agreed that if something was not done very soon Willie would lose both his wife and his baby.

Lady's hair ... tangled there ... never share ... never share ... beware, beware ...

The weather seemed to imitate the agony Willie's lady was enduring but that evening, unable to sleep, Willie braved the tempest and walked the castle, every nook and cranny of it, not knowing where he was or where he was going.

On the battlements he met Blind Betty, an old crone who had been employed by the family as a servant long ago in his father's day but who now made some kind of a living by telling fortunes and casting spells. She had known Willie since the moment of his birth so took the liberty of approaching him and speaking openly.

'If you want to save the life of your wife and have her safely deliver your son then do everything I tell you,' she said. 'Do it carefully and in every detail.'

Then she laid out a plan: 'You must get a cake of wax and shape it into the form of a baby and put glass beads in its head for eyes. Dress that baby in your family's finest Christening robe and then announce to one and all that the baby is born and everyone is invited to the Christening ceremony. Be sure to deliver the message to your mother yourself and when you do, stand close and mark well what she says when she hears.'

So, the next morning Willie went into the market and bought a large cake of wax and shaped it into the form of a baby. He put glass beads into its head for eyes and dressed it in the family's finest Christening robe and, from the gate tower, announced to all and sundry that the baby was born and everyone was invited to the Christening ceremony. Willie took the message to his mother himself.

When she heard the words she grew pale and trembled, and then turned red and shook with rage. She stamped her feet, jumped in the air, threw herself on the ground, tore her hair and ripped her clothing. Then started to mutter under her breath, a rant that rose to a scream:

'Who's undone the nine witch knots that I tangled in her locks?
And who took out the combs of care that lay among the lady's hair?
And who has loosed her left-foot shoe that did bind up her care and woe
And who has killed the Master Kid that lay beneath the lady's bed?
And who has felled the magic tree and let the lady lighter be?'

When he heard this Willie ran home.

... Willie undid the nine witch knots that tangled in his lady's locks.

... And Willie took out the combs of care that lay among the lady's hair.

... And Willie loosed her left-foot shoe that did bind up her care and woe.

... And Willie killed the Master Kid that lay beneath the lady's bed.

... And Willie felled the magic tree and let the lady lighter be.

As soon as the final task was complete the Lady Regat went into labour. And I am pleased to announce that both mother and child are doing well.

Professor Francis James Child found only one version of this song ('Willie's Lady': Child 6/ Roud 220/Ballad Index C006) and no tune, so it might never have been sung widely as a traditional song. It is, however, quite well known in the folk revival. Scottish singer Ray Fisher (sister to the better-known Archie) set the words to the Breton tune 'Son Ar Chistr' (Song of Cider) and this was recorded by Martin Carthy on his Crown of Horn LP in 1976. That setting has now become the standard version.

The ballad tells one of those stories that occur in various parts of Europe: there are Danish and Swedish versions and it has parallels in Greek mythology with the birth of Heracles.

The words, as published by Child, tell only a small part of the story – it leaps in midway. We are given none of the back-story and no idea of what happens afterwards. In many ways this is a strength and is one of the things I love about ballads – you are left to imagine your own version and your reading of it might be very different to mine.

I have never considered singing it but I love the story. I have expanded and explained it a bit but have, hopefully, left enough space and mystery for your imagination to work.

7

The Dark Queen of Bamburgh

A Retelling of the Ballad 'The Laidly Worm of Spindlestone Heugh' by Malcolm Green

Her breath grew strang, her hair grew lang,
And twisted thrice about the tree,
And all the people, far and near,
Thought that a savage beast was she.

ANON, Northumbria

There was once a king of Bamburgh Castle, whose wife had died, leaving him with a son, Childe Wynd, and a daughter, Margaret. The two of them played in the sands below the castle with the vast, bleak North Sea as their companion, ever enticing them to dream of distant places.

One day Childe Wynd announced that he was going to explore the land beyond the horizon and see what treasure he might find. He embraced his sister, saying, 'I shall return soon with great gifts for you that will make you the most beautiful woman on earth.'

'Be bold my brother, I am waiting for you,' she replied.

But the truth was that Margaret was already the most beautiful of women, with yellow hair that rippled down her back like autumn corn and eyes that sparkled as blue as summer flax. People were proud to have her as their princess and she, in turn, had time for everyone. It was she who controlled the mighty keys to the castle.

Her father, a king of great power, one day announced that he would be away for some time. Margaret looked into his eyes and understood that soon there would be a new queen. She bade him farewell and assumed charge of the castle.

Margaret's stature grew as she walked through the streets of the town, a smile on her lips and her body swaying like the sea itself. She greeted everyone from the peasant farmers to the local chieftains, listening to difficulties and resolving disputes. She was particularly courteous to the native Britons, who mistrusted their Anglo-Saxon rulers.

One day news came of the king's return. People lined the streets, straining to see the carriage as it traversed the steep path to the castle gates. They clicked their tongues with appreciation when they caught glimpses of the new bride, finely dressed and with dark skin, black hair and green eyes. Margaret stood by the castle gates, firm and gracious, with two of her loyal, local chieftains standing by her side. They cheered as the carriage approached. Then one of the chiefs looked into the green eyes of the new woman and turned to his companion saying, 'She may be beautiful but I don't care for her as I do our Lady Margaret.'

Amongst the hubbub the new queen read the chief's lips and understood much; she immediately felt her authority was threatened. 'Well, your beautiful Margaret will not last for long,' she muttered to herself.

Margaret curtsied to the new queen as she alighted from the carriage at the castle doors.

'The castle is yours, mother,' she said sweetly as she handed over the keys.

'Thank you, my dear,' replied the new queen, making Margaret feel slightly nervous with the strained smile on her tight lips.

The king noticed nothing of the exchange. He was too entranced by the beauty of his new wife to have any notion that she was a practitioner of the black arts.

The new queen decided to take matters in hand and ensure her authority that very night. She knew that questions would be asked if she simply poisoned the princess, so she decided to deal with Margaret by other means. No sooner had she had been shown her room than she unlaced a worn bull's skin bag and took out various phials from which she prepared a concoction. When she was finished, she poured the potion into a small glass jar, leaned over and muttered the words of a charm.

She carefully slipped it into her bodice.

That evening, at their very first dinner together, the new queen waited until the company's attention was drawn to a convenient alter-cation in the corridor and she poured the liquid into Margaret's glass.

The following morning Margaret did not appear for breakfast. People called for her and searched for her but she could not be found; her bed chamber empty and her sheets unused. The king was dis-traught and ordered the search to be extended to the castle grounds. Nothing was found save a piece of red material, from one of her dresses, caught on the cliffs beneath the castle. Had she fallen, it was unlikely? She knew these cliffs so well and there was no sign of a body. Perhaps she had been taken by the fairy folk? No one knew, least of all the king who fell into a state of deep grief.

Then, one day, one of the local chieftains came to the castle, asking only for the king.

He bowed low. 'Sire,' he said, 'There is a laidly worm on Spindlestone Heugh, causing terror amongst the citizens.'

'A laidly worm, a dragon at Spindlestone Heugh?'

'Yes sire, its tail is wound around the Bridlestone. Each day it grows another foot, its eyes staring out towards the Farne Islands and roaring as if in great distress.'

'Are you drunk, man?' said the king. 'You'll be strung up, if you are!'

'No sir, the beast is true, any man from Spindlestone will tell you so and it has a voracious appetite. The only thing that will calm it down is milk. The farmers are pouring seven gallons each day into a stone trough and still the beast grows.'

'What damage is it doing?' said the king, incredulous.

'It seems to have no interest in harming folk, apart from the cost of the milk, which is dear sire. Only its venomous breath is poisoning and scorching all the pasture for miles around; it will ruin the whole country! Indeed, I have little grass left for my cattle. The farmers are in despair.'

'Have you not men that can rid us of this thing?'

'Many men have tried with pitchforks and lances but nothing will enter its scaly skin.'

'I will send soldiers at once.'

'I believe,' said the chieftain, 'that only your son, Childe Wynd, can rid us of this beast.'

'Then he shall be summoned,' said the king.

Childe Wynd, however, was already on his way across the sea from France, booty filling the coffers off many chests.

The new queen kept her ears close to the ground and when the first sight of sails was seen on the far horizon, she took herself to a place on the windy cliff-top. She had no desire to have the king's son meddling into her business. She looked out across the grey, steely ocean and used her power to conjure up a storm, throwing her arms into the air and shrieking into the waves. And the sea and sky responded; a fierce wind whipped out into the ocean, creating gigantic breakers that pounded onto the rocks and shore.

Try as he might, Childe Wynd could not battle through it. The captain of the boat turned to him. 'That is no ordinary storm; see how the sky is still clear, there is witchcraft in it! We must return and build a boat of rowan wood.'

So they arrived back in France where men sawed and jointed planks of rowan to create a new boat.

It was several months later that the rowan wood boat hoisted its red sails and left for Budle Bay.

Again the witch queen was waiting and again she summoned a storm but even though it was more powerful than the one before, the boat sliced through the waves to reach the shore. 'Witchcraft!' shouted the captain, as Childe Wynd jumped onto the sands of the bay.

Ducks and wading birds rose in a frenzy above his head, wheeling around in the wind.

Above, on the rocks of Spindlestone, the laidly worm watched. Then very quietly it slid through gorse and birch, towards the bay. Childe Wynd saw it coming and drew his sword. But the creature made no sign of defence or retreat. It crossed the mud straight towards him, its huge head looking down from a scaly neck.

Chlide Wynd looked up into the beast's eyes and raised his blade. But in that instant he noticed something strange. It had eyes the colour of flax blossom that evoked a familiar yearning memory in him. He hesitated.

A strange guttural, rumbling noise came from deep in the worm's belly and it spoke:

> *'Quit thy sword and bend thy bow,*
> *And give me kisses three;*
> *If I'm not won ere the sun goes down,*
> *Won I shall never be.'*

Despite the voice was deep, he knew it, though he was not sure from where ...

Childe Wynd sheathed his sword, leaned forward and, to the amazement of all watching, kissed the worm three times on its stinking lips.

Slowly the mighty beast transformed: scales started to fall from its body, its mighty head retracted and its limbs became pale and soft.

There before him stood his sister, Margaret, her eyes wild and frightened. Childe Wynd wrapped his red cloak around her naked body.

'Thank you, my brother,' she said softly, 'I knew you must come in time.' Then her voice hardened like steel. 'It is the new queen who did this.'

Together they walked along the soft sand toward Bamburgh Castle and climbed up the cliffs they knew so well. The queen and king were supping on sweetmeats when the brother and sister entered the dining room.

The king's face lit up.

The queen's drained of colour; words stumbled out of her mouth. 'Oh, you're back, you must ...' She made as if to leave.

'Stay,' said Childe Wynd.

'You've done enough damage,' said Margaret. 'It is time for you to receive the blessing of a laidly worm.'

And as the word 'blessing' came from Margaret's lips, the witch queen began to shrivel, her skin becoming wrinkled, warty and

brown, until there, in her place, squatting on the cold palace floor, was a toad.

Childe Wynd flicked it with his foot out of the window and into a flowerbed.

And if I'm not mistaken there is a great toad lolloping around the castle grounds to this day.

Bamburgh and the nearby Spindlestone Heugh are dramatic places along a wild coastline facing out to the North Sea. The story was originally a ballad collected by Revd Robert Lambert, vicar of Norham, in 1778 (he claimed it to be taken from a ballad by Duncan Fraser, a Cheviot bard in 1270. There is some debate as to whether this is true, or whether Lambert simply relocated the ballad, 'Kemp Owyne' (Child 34/Roud 3912), originally set in Wales, to the Northumberland coastline). It origins may, however, go back to the sixth century when Spindlestone was a site of pagan worship and maidens thrown into the sea as offerings to the Gods. King Ida, the first Anglo-Saxon king of Northumberland, was said to have been enchanted by one such maiden, a Bethoc witch with green eyes and dark hair.

The verse about 'bending the bow' is taken from: William James Henderson's Notes on the Folklore of the Northern Counties and Borders *(1866).*

8

What Women Most Desire

A Retelling of the Ballad 'The Marriage of Gawain' by Simon Heywood

> *Her nose was crooked and turnd outward,*
> *Her mouth stood foule a-wry;*
> *A worse formed lady than shee was,*
> *Neuer man saw with his eye.*

ANON

North of Penrith, the M6 motorway runs among the rolling green fields of the lower Eden Valley, towards Carlisle. You could be forgiven for failing to notice that the motorway here runs through a land of mystery. Within a dozen miles, at Croglin, you'll find the haunt of one of England's very few known vampires, and many other marvels. But if you were to take the A6, and turn off it at High Hesket, or come the other way from Armathwaite station, you would find yourself passing a patch of rough woodland. You could pass it a dozen times and never look twice at it. There would be little to tell you that it was once the bed of a lake. But it was.

In the old days, long before the busy Victorians drained it, it was a famous place of ill omen, and it had more than one name. Some called it Laykebrait, 'the lake that sounds'; but any story that lies behind that name has long since been forgotten. Others called it Tarn Wadling or Tarn Wathelin, and it was by that name that the lake found fame in the tales of the great King Arthur, for there Arthur first found his personal limits as a king, while Gawain, his nephew and favourite knight, found his bride.

And this is the story of how it happened.

Arthur went riding out one day from his court at Carlisle in the good Old North, that his forefather Leil had built. As the king was returning home from a poor day's hunting, skirting the shores of Tarn Wathelin in the gathering dusk, a giant ogre leapt out of the shadows as if from nowhere and attacked the king with a club. Kings, in those days as in these, are slow to show fear, so Arthur returned battle heartily, with scarcely a second thought. Before long, the ogre had beaten him to the ground. The king surrendered and begged for mercy with every ounce of eloquence lying at his command.

'Mercy you shall have, Arthur, king and warrior,' the ogre rasped, 'but on my terms alone. For if you wish to escape with your life, you shall swear, by your throne, and your kingdom, and the glory of your father's name, that, this day twelve months from now you will come once again to this very place, and give me the head from your shoulders, and the crown that rests upon it, unless, on that day, you can answer the riddle that now I shall ask.' He was a remarkably articulate ogre.

Arthur swore that he would do it, and told him to ask his riddle.

'My riddle is this,' the ogre said. 'What is it that women most desire?'

Strictly speaking, this was not a riddle so much as a question, but Arthur was not in a position to quibble terms, and was not in any case feeling particularly competent to venture an answer to the question off the cuff. So he agreed the ogre's terms and was thankful to make his escape back to Carlisle.

In those dark times, Arthur's court was the glory of the world for chivalry and learning, and all that year Arthur went up and down it, and put the ogre's question to wizard and warrior, scholar and knight and priest, men of the world and men of book-learning. What is it, he asked them all, that women most desire? He sought the answer in vain. Perhaps he should have asked a woman.

Kings, in those days as in these, are men of their word at any rate, so when the year was up, Arthur quietly set his affairs in order as best he could, and rode out with a heavy heart towards Tarn Wathelin in the gathering dusk. Never had he been more certain of anything than he was that day of his own imminent death.

But before the king could come to the Tarn, it happened that a mist descended. He lost his way in the mist and before long he found himself in the shadow of a great crag, which he could not remember ever having seen before. Nor was that all, for faintly yet clearly to be glimpsed in the mist was the most extraordinary creature the king had ever seen. The figure was rocking and singing in a cracked voice. She seemed to be a woman, more or less, but age had bent her right over like a wheel, and so frail did she seem to be that Arthur thought the mist itself might have billowed straight through her. She was dressed in filthy rags, and her hooked nose and chin, warty and tufted, met in the space before her face, like the points of a great pair of blunted shears. Two long ropes of greasy hair hung down either side over sunken cheeks, and between them, where her mouth should have been, a single, staring, bloodshot eye was set, while on her wrinkled brow, where her eyes should have been, there gaped her bleary, shrivelled mouth, with one mossy tooth still clinging to denuded gums. She was laughing as she sang, and kicking up her heels, and she pointed to the king as he rode past.

'Look at the fool going to his death,' she cackled, 'for want of the knowledge I could give him. If only he would ask it!'

The king's ears pricked up at once, and he spurred his horse towards the foot of the crag.

'Fair lady,' the king said, for kings were still courteous in those days, 'what you say, alas, is true enough; but if you do know the answer, how shall I ask you for it?'

A sudden glint lit up the hag's eye.

'Bargain for it,' she said.

'What will you take for it?' the king asked frankly.

'My choice of your knights for my husband, at Carlisle next Midsummer's Day,' the hag said at once.

The king considered a moment.

'That is in my power to offer you,' he admitted.

'Then I choose Gawain,' the hag said at once.

'He's single. He's yours!' Arthur replied, greatly relieved. 'You have my word on it.'

The hag kicked up her heels and screeched.

'Then approach, O King!'

The king approached, and leaned in and down, and the hag strained until her loathsome lips were almost touching the King's ear, and she whispered, 'Ask the riddle.'

In a faltering tone, Arthur asked, 'What is it that women most desire?'

The words she whispered in reply were these: 'Women want what women want.'

And before the king could answer, she kicked up her heels again and vanished in the mist.

'Gawain!' cried the cracked, ghostly voice as it faded in the mist. 'Midsummer's Day!'

And, with that, Arthur was alone.

With a heart even heavier than before, Arthur rode alone on to Tarn Wathelin, half-hoping that the ogre might have missed the day.

There was no time to make further debate of the riddle, and evening was drawing in. But, sure enough, he saw the dark shape looming out of the dusk. His heart sank even further as the ogre stepped out of the mist, brandishing his club, a great knotted oak torn almost whole from the earth, and stripped of leaves and branches: a terrible thing, a certain instrument of shameful and agonising death. Arthur remembered that club very well. King and ogre faced each other, in the dusk by the shore.

'So, Arthur, king and warrior,' the ogre boomed, 'you have kept your word, and kept the day. Have you learned the right answer to my riddle?'

'I shall tell you the best answer I have,' the king said gallantly, 'but its rightness is not for me to judge. But if my best answer wants rightness in your eyes, son of Cain, child of Gogmagog, then know that this day, in fulfilment of my oath, my head shall be yours, and my crown with it. My answer is this: "Women want what women want".'

There was a short silence.

The ogre's face fell, and his brow clouded, and he let the oaken club fall with a crash, and crashed off into the mist, bellowing disconsolately, and tearing at the trees, and pounding the rocks with his fists until they echoed. His last, despairing words were these: 'You've been talking to my sister!'

Arthur saw him no more. He rode home to Carlisle.

The great oak-tree club lay till it rotted.

Gawain was Arthur's nephew. Many was the old counsellor who looked fondly on the young man as hope of the realm. Many a young knight secretly cursed his own destiny because he had been born as his own self, and not as the flawless and graceful Sir Gawain. Many was the pillow drenched nightly with tears as it cradled some poor maiden's head, wreathed as she lay in the lonely watches of the night with hopeless dreams of the unguessable depths of Gawain's capacity for earthly love.

Gawain himself would have had to be remarkably stupid to notice nothing of any of this, but, in fact, he seemed to show no awareness at all of the effect he had on other people. He was a quiet, affable young man whom some thought unusually arrogant, and others unusually humble. His interests seemed confined to serving the king, in battle and tournament and adventure. He was known as a good team player. He seemed in no hurry to take a wife.

Arthur knew very well that even a king cannot keep a secret for long at a court, so, as soon as was decently possible, he summoned Gawain to a private audience. He was determined to tell Gawain everything and appeal to the young warrior's loyalty and discretion. Gawain watched as Arthur dismissed his servants.

'Nephew,' Arthur began. 'Do you want the good news, or the bad news?'

'I will hear the news willingly, in any order,' the young man replied.

By the end of the interview, Arthur had told Gawain the truth, or most of it. Gawain gave a small shrug and seemed to consider for a moment. But he said very little. He left the king's presence and the following day he behaved as if nothing had changed.

Shortly after that, the rumour did indeed begin to circulate that Gawain had accepted betrothal to the bride of the king's choosing, in some bargain with the mysterious forces which never lurked too far from the gates of the courts of old Albion. Many a hard word was breathed against Arthur behind his back, but on Midsummer's Day, the whole court was packed and chattering excitedly, to see the young hero's bride make her appearance.

And into the court, on a white palfrey, the loathsome hag came riding, with her flesh faint, and her back bent, and her eye where her mouth should be, and her mouth where her eyes should be. Through the thick silence she rode, and then through the chuckling and tittering from mouth to mouth behind hand and veil and psalter, until she reined in her horse before her husband-to-be.

Gawain and his bride looked on one another for the first time.

In the silence Gawain stepped forward and took the hag's twisted hand in his own hand, and helped her from her horse, and before the whole court he bade her welcome to Carlisle, and easily and naturally he asked after her health, and gravely hoped that she had had a pleasant and comfortable journey.

The strange wedding was soon over, the couple were shown to the bridal chamber, and the servants closed the door on them and discreetly withdrew. The hag fixed Gawain with her one bleary eye, and asked him to turn away and face the wall while she made herself ready for bed. Gawain faced the wall, turning over many anxious thoughts, until he found himself wondering, as many husbands have wondered before and since, what 'making oneself ready' could possibly involve, that it could take so long. Then a voice told him that he could turn round now. Gawain turned, and saw.

Exactly what he saw in that moment he never revealed, for he was Gawain, and would have sooner died than speak of such things. But, as he himself told the story afterwards, what he saw struck him to the core with such overwhelming love that it seemed suddenly to him that his whole life until that moment had been nothing but a dreamless sleep, from which he was now, at last, ready to awake. And though he was a young man, having as yet little real fear of death, Gawain, knowing well, as everyone knows, that one day indeed he must die, knew too from that instant onwards he need never now fear what all young men fear the most – the prospect of dying without ever having truly lived – for he was alive at last, and he knew it.

He managed to ask what had happened; and she gave a laugh whose lightest cadence fell more sweetly on Gawain's ears than ever had the music of the court.

'Husband,' she laughed, 'what did they teach you, here in the schools? Did they teach you that women are born with their eyes where their mouths should be, or their mouths where their eyes should be? Do I think I was born so? No, husband. We were under spells and curses, my brother and I. The curse was this: that we must appear loathsome and strange, telling nobody why, or how, until the finest knight of Arthur's court should freely choose me for his wife. Those who cursed us did that to taunt us, thinking it could never come to pass; but now it has, and the curse is half-broken.'

Well, thought Gawain, that's good.

'For you alone can see me now as I truly am, in my own form,' the lady went on sadly, 'although, to the eyes of the court, I can never be other than the loathsome hag which first they saw yesterday. And so it must be for the rest of our days.'

That's not so good, Gawain thought.

'Hang on a bit,' he protested. He hesitated a moment, and went on, 'I barely understand a word of this ... but, if I'm following you – you're you, now, but they'll never see you, they'll only ever see ... '

'A hag,' she repeated. 'Yes. Loathsome.'

'But—' he hesitated again. 'I can't put you through all that. How could I? How could I stand by and let you suffer all the laughing, and the sniggering, and the gossiping, as you go to face them in the form that – pleases them so little? The form in which they saw you first? People here think I'm not very observant. Perhaps I'm not. But I see what goes on. I cannot put my wedded wife to that daily shame.' He drew himself up resolutely. 'I will seek the King's permission to retire from court life.'

'Perhaps we must,' she replied smoothly. 'But – there are other means at your disposal, husband,' she added.

'Other means?'

'You can choose for the whole court to see me, in the form in which you see me now.'

'Well, let them then, of course!' Gawain nearly said, but she held up a hand and silenced him.

'But then,' she went on sadly, 'to you – and to you alone –– I must always be that loathsome hag. Such is the half-curse that remains. And such is your choice: a hag by day still I must be, or else a hag by night: and it is you who must make the choice.'

Gawain balked a moment and she laughed sadly.

'Is it so hard to choose,' she said, 'between your pleasure, and my shame?'

There was silence.

At last, Gawain spoke.

'Hard? It is impossible,' he said bluntly. 'Lady, now I have seen the truth, it will live with me forever; no curse could blight it, and I would wed you gladly again a thousand times for its sake. If so you please, then let the court see the truth in its turn by day; or let it be me that sees it by night. It is no matter. It is your truth. It is your choice.'

She looked at him in wonder.

'Well, did I choose you for my husband,' she exclaimed, 'for your heart has answered the riddle that Arthur could scarcely grasp, for all the help I could give him; and so the curse is broken not by halves, but wholly, and my brother and I shall have peace at last. Gawain, you gave me freedom to choose, and with the gift I am myself again, in all times and places, by days and nights together, in court and chamber alike. So let us not speak of retirement from court. It will do the court a deal of good, I think, to see people as they truly are.'

Gawain was speechless with joy and wonder, but she only smiled, and her eyes glittered, and she said, 'Husband, I thank you for your patience. Now, at last, I am ready for bed.'

When morning came, they rose and dressed, and went to court. All Carlisle wondered at them, but Arthur smiled, and kept the two of them especially in his favour forever afterwards. In time the matter was all but forgotten. But not quite: for, though Arthur fell in the end, and his court met its downfall with him, still the tale of Gawain's wedding to Lady Ragnell is told today, though Tarn Wathelin itself is drained and dry, and its bed lies under the trees by the side of the road, between High Hesket and Armathwaite, between Penrith and Carlisle in the lower Eden Valley.

'The Marriage of Sir Gawain' (Child 31) comes from the Percy Folio. Beyond that, its authorship is unknown, and parts of the original story were once used to light fires and lost forever. The tale is related to the fifteenth-century 'The Wedding of Sir Gawain and Dame Ragnell' and other medieval romances. I've known the story for a long time and have been telling it live for a couple of years. It's one of those stories where the deeper you dig, the more you find.

9

The Droll of Ann Tremellan

A Retelling of the Ballad 'Ann Tremellan'
by Alan M. Kent

In Cornwall, boy Johnny was born and bred,
In Cornwall was his dwelling,
And there he courted a pretty maid,
Her name was Ann Tremellan.

ANON, Cornwall

In termen eze passiez ...

What? You don't understand? Alright, I'll begin again. Let me tell you the droll of Ann Tremellan.

'Es, in times gone by, back in the days of *bal* and *brythel* (perhaps you'd say *mine* and *mackerel* now), the Cornish (the old West Britons) named their world with very different words and sounds. They named their life – and they named their death (which in they days, was frequent and often) – with the old tongue, the Troyance tongue: the one that some still spoke.

This time I tell of was a time of crossover and blending, of quickly shifting sands, when the Cornish language co-existed with that new mouthful of difficulty called English. You spoke English to the Squire an' the Mine Cap'n, but on the smallholding or down mine, you always used Cornish – same as generations of bewdies and buggers before. There was no doubt: it was slipping though. Some days, boy Johnny Pearce, aged just twenty, found ee had more words in his gob from over the Tamar than those nearer Land's End (what people on the Lizard still called *Pedn-an-wlase*). 'Twas like you couldn' stop ut you. It seeped its way in – like damp coming up through carn granite. It was there everywhere you looked.

The damp I knew well. See me an' Johnny were pards over mine. We worked tribute over Wheal Vor. Tribute is when a man an' a boy pair up, and work the seam together. What you make is moastly your own, but the mine d'take a percentage. 'Es, over Carleen is where we worked in the parish of Breage. Top of the Lizard we be, but go directly south and you'm in Landewednack, one small step further – and you'm in the sea. That be the southernmost part – what the old books call Predannack. They d'say thaas' what the Romans called ut – on their way t'the Cassiterides or the 'islands of tin'. See, mining's what we'm built fur. 'Tis in the blood.

Boring and digging at the stope is brave mazed and mucky work. You d'get proper lagged up. And it d'smell of the earth. It gets in ee. In yer bones like. Never goes away. Down under though, your pard is all that matters. Ee d'look after you and you d'look after ee. There's danger there every day see: charges, fuses, collapses, timber failing, solars opening up. You have t'mind your footing. You mind your head too. Felt hats are essential. Bent over double, always. There's no room fur error. You'm hunched up proper. It d'shimmer down there though – canopies of minerals and crystals, as if Heaven's just above ee. You d'hope God's standing right next to ee when you'm down on the fifty fathom level.

'The Devil's proab'ly a bit closer,' said Johnny as we went a-steppin' down the man-engine's greasy ladders. One slip was enough t'send ee tumbling inta the void. Ee was right by what ee said. Underground you could imagine imps and demons awaiting with hooves and horns, and hear the screaming souls of the eternally damned being tortured.

I'd knawn Johnny a goodly time you. We went school together. Worked the fields too. Shared tools. Drunk the same bowls of herbie-beer when turning over of the hay each summer. And down Rinsey beach we jumped – 'es, bollock-naked – inta the waves. Because I'm telling you the tale, and because, well, now, this is a different time, I'm using English, but back then, 'twas all Cornish between me and he.

Whether 'twas pick and gad that passed between us, or charge or drill bit, it mattered not. We had our code; our way of working the rock. That code was the language.

Each core was long. We did twelve hours of suffering underground. Saturdays we worked home: planted cabbages, turnip, fattened a pig and kept a few hens. 'Course, Sundays was always chapel. Chapel, chapel, chapel. Starched collars that itch, an' your best bib an' tucker. 'Es, we'd all traipse in t'get a bollocking from Wesley's words. Ee was a good man though, a godly man, like they d'say. Do all the good you can. By all the means you can. In all the ways you can. I have always tried t'follow tha'. And I believe Johnny did too.

So we sung his hymns and said the Lord's Prayer – in Cornish and in English.

'*Agan Tas-ny, us yn nef,*
    Benygys re bo dha Hanow ...'
'Our Father which art in heaven,
    Hallowed be they name ...'

And then, when we wuz at prayer, I s'pause thaas' when I nawticed Johnny's look. 'Twudn' much. But ut said enough. There's this maid see. I knawed of ut all along. I knawed Johnny was keen on she. 'Er name was Ann Tremellan. Some pretty maid. From over Germoe way, they d'say. Faace like an angel. A warm body on her that you wudn't want t'let go of on a cold winter's night. Some bewdie she was. An' 'er eyes – well, 'er eyes were like raw tin, always glistening back at ee. Her lips were a like a pierced cherry – ready to suck and savour. I knaw thaas' why Johnny fell fur she. But there was somethun' about she too – somethun' cruel. Like she knew what she did to many a man and boy.

She knawed her power.

Knawed her witchery.

She had ut in spades.

'Twudn' long before Johnny was waitin' for she each Sunday. 'Ee'd mill about seein' ef ee could catch her eye. And the more ee waited, the more she nawticed. I mean, she could've 'ad er pick, that one. Plenty ov men would've walked t'Temple Moors an' back for she. Johnny didn' say much though. Ee just kept lookin'. See, that way, his keen eyes pierced her soul. An' once that've happened, well, maids, they can't resist. They'm putty in your hands then.

A month later, Johnny was walkin' her home wudn' a. An' 'es, 'twas a walk that took double the time ut shud. I laughed, like a pig pissing.

I had un goin' back down stope on Monday mornin'.

'The Tremellan maid then, is ut?' I said when we wuz havin' our crowst.

'I d'reckon.'

'You an' she a-courtin' then?'

'Might be,' ee said, biting off of a bravish big corner of his pasty.

'Do 'er mawther and feyther knaw?'

Ee didn' answer. So I s'paused not yet.

'"You'd best square ut with Mr Tremellan," I said, an' warned un there an' then. "Ee' want t'knaw o your intentions".'

Ee was silent. No words came from un in Cornish or in English. And that, I fear, was an omen.

'You hear me Johnny?'

'Will do, Grammer,' at last, says ee t'me.

After tha', well, Johnny and me wudn' quite the same. There wuz no time fur dips in the blustery sea down Rinsey. Ee was too taken with she. There were sweetheart cards an' tokens. He asked t'take 'er Penzance fair, and she went with un fur devilment. And ut being summer, she would meet un after core. They'd walk up moor or go down shore. And Johnny was different. Like as ef ee'd become a man overnight. Now he'd shave an' grease down his hair. Up washroom there was never enough soap. I knawed 'ee wanted t'be clean fur she. Ee never wanted muck nor mud to get on her cream dresses or white bonnets.

Now, this Ann Tremellan wudn't long in leaving school.

'What d'she plan t'do?' I asked of un.

'She'll work bal I s'pect for now,' he said. 'Cob ore an' tha'. She can read an' write though, proper good. Says she wants to be a governess.'

I see'd she one day a-fore the pump house door. She knew me well enough.

'Hope you'm lookin' after my pard. Some boy there, you.'

'I knaw,' she said.

'Dun't ee be leadun' un a merry dance. Ee's some tickled up ass with you.'

She looked at me proper cakey-like.

'I wun't,' she said succinctly. 'It's Johnny I want to be a-wedded to.'

'Tell un then,' I said, 'or ee wun't think ut's true.'

'And Annie dear, keep your eyes off other men – is that clear? I've seen the way you look sometimes …'

'I've only eyes for Johnny,' she said, clenching her fists.

'Good,' I replied. 'For love should be there both in life and death.'

I hardly knew what prophetic words I'd said.

All ov that comed back to bite at me. 'Twudn' long after I see'd she. 'Es. 'Twas the merry month of May. Breage was celebrating the Maying. A dance through the village and service in the church, but we wuz back mine still, hard at work. Other than ut being May Day, all was normal – thinking back. There was no warning see. Sometimes miners say they can sniff danger. Either that or your candle blaws out. We was making way see, along the level. Stoping back good, we were. Five feet in since crib alone. The ore was coming off lovely you, so we'd bucketed it up for the trammers. But as soon as we'd rested shovels an' touched pipe fur a bit, the roof rumbled and – Christ – it fell clean down. 'Twas one hell of a shock, I'n tell ee. We'd worked the stope all week and timbered it up good. But what comed down wudn' nothun' light-weight. A ton or two at least engulfed we. I was fair caked in rock an' dust but Johnny, well, ee was down on the floor under ut all. There was blood pouring, and 'ell, his chest was caved right in. The rock-fall must've broke every rib. The poor bugger was moaning and groaning on.

I maked 'iss and moved all the burden that I could. The rest of the core comed down the level, and helped me get un up and out. I could see from their faces though that they didn' think he'd pull through. See, even when brought up t'grass, Johnny cudn' breathe right. I'n see un now, laid out on the pickings and all around the green buds were swelling. It had to be said: death was part pained on his face. The other side seemed t'be stealin' ov his heart.

Later, we got un home but things didn' look good. His mawther placed un on his bed, in his room upstairs. I sat there, listening to un, and over and over again, all 'ee cried was her name: Ann Tremellan. Ann Tremellan. On it rumbled, like a drum.

'Annie, Annie. Please come to me,' ee'd say 'til his lips were bone dry.

'They've called fur she,' I said. 'She'll be on her way.'

But another day passed before word came that she wuz stanking on over.

'The better I shall be,' he said, 'to see my bonny Ann Tremellan.'

'I know boy,' I said. But in truth, inside, there was a dread. It was that cruelty she showed. Like as if she wished un t'suffer. She was the kind of chield that pulled wings off butterflies and then watched them reel. There was a darkness in her heart.

Then finally news came up from Johnny's mawther, that Ann Tremellan had arrived. Slowly, slowly, she came up the stairs and slowly, she came beside him. When Johnny seen of er, I traced a smile on his face. Coldly though, she held his hand – as if it were the right thing to do.

'Oh Annie,' I heard him say, 'I had such hopes for you an' me. And now look at me. Crushed and staved in …'

I seen her eyes fall over his body then. She sat for an hour with un, and held his hand. And each stroke of her was like another crushing blow. In all that time, she said nothing, but these words: 'Young man. I think you're a-dying.'

I stood her up. I turned to face her straight. 'Can ee not say anything a bit more encouraging?'

She gaked up at me, proud still, as if hurt hadn't been felt. 'I only told the truth,' she said. 'No point in lying.'

She sat again and once more reached for his hand. I knew Johnny's kind heart was breaking.

Breathless and gasping, he said to she, 'O lovely maid, come pity me. I knaw I'm on my death-bed lying …'

I wanted she to comfort him. Perhaps one final kiss upon his lips. Maybe words of Cornish to help him be at peace. But no, this Ann Tremellan stayed as hard as stone. She was a menhir of hate, a gnarled boulder of despondency.

'If on your death-bed you do lie, what needs the tale that you're telling? I cannot keep you from your death ...'

He gazed at her, wanting more – so wanting her to help him pass.

But instead, she said just one bitter word more, 'Farewell!'

She brushed past me and went quickly down the stairs. He'd been discarded as if a piece of common flookan. Johnny was gazing still, up to his heavenly fate. Ee hardly knew she'd gone. Minutes later, ee was still calling fur she, even though she was now halfway to Germoe.

'Annie, dear Annie!' came the call, over and over again.

'She's gone boy,' I said.

At that, he turned his face to the wall. On the whitewash he saw nothun'. And that he knew, was now his fate. Death was in the room with a pack of cruel cards, and was with him dealing. Death had all the Aces too.

I watched. I listened. I leaned in close. I could hear no sound or breathe, and then, just as I thought he'd been snatched, he managed to say this to me. His words did echo hers, and still surprisingly perhaps, ee felt love for her – the one who had left him a-dying.

'Farewell, my friends and neighbours all. Promise me; just be kind to Ann Tremellan.'

And with that her love, my pard, this young boy was cut down by Death's decisive scythe. On the bed, he lay like a broken corn-sheath, gathered at harvest. He'd gone too soon though. He was just in the Maying of his life.

'Gone?' asked his mawther.

'Ee's gone,' I said.

The tears came then.

'I see that trollop didn' stay long.'

'No,' I said, 'She've better things t'do than care for the injured or the dying.'

On his eyes I placed two pennies and said a prayer in Cornish. Hopefully in heaven he'll find others there who speak that tongue. They can converse just as they should.

Two days later, ee was buried in Breage churchyard. His resting place sits on a line running from Wheal Vor straight to Germoe. His head is in the west. I knawed that would be what he would have wanted.

There was a good many there fur'n mind. Both chapel and church. Cap'n and owners of Wheal Vor too. 'Course, they said there'd be safer ways of workin' the levels. But that sentiment will soon go. This is Cornwall boy. Half the trees are underground propping up the earth. We'll climb into any hole – dangerous or not – if there's a shilling or two to be made. Soon his dying will be forgot. We'll carry on turning the earth inside out.

Now, 'twas raining the day of his funeral. In fact, 'twas enting down. One of they there sea mists comed in right over. Breage and half of the Lizard. I tell ee, although I might be wrong, I swear I saw Ann Tremellan – in black this time – a-standing by the lych-gate, as Johnny was given back to the earth. 'Twas only a glance, and when I looked again, she'd gone.

You d'hear stories. Well, this is Cornwall, and we'm full ov ut. But so it went that day, Ann Tremellan walked her way back to Germoe, but so 'tis said, her heart was struck with such sorrow that when she got home, she said straight to her mam, 'Oh mother, mother, make my bed, for I knaw I shall die tomorrow!' Now her mother wudn' mazed a bit by that, but sometimes the truth is stranger than fiction. For that Ann Tremellan, that cruel girl, who seemed to curse all, the next day was found alone, dead in her bed. She was as still as alabaster stone.

Before that, so her sisters said, she had called out in the night.

'What did she say?' I asked. 'I bet it was curt and quick.'

'Oh no,' says them, 'She talked of love and what ut meant.'

'Really?'

''Es. And then … she said farewell to us maidens all …'

'There's more?'

One sister nodded, wiping away her tears, and said, 'She told we to shun the fault she fell into and take warning at the fall of our dear sister, Ann Tremellan.'

And so it seemed, at the end, Ann had repented what she'd done before, and how she treated her dear Johnny Pearce.

'Fate has a weird sense of dealing,' was all I could say. So poor Ann and poor Johnny had no wedding day. But perhaps in their peace I find some pity.

I'm old now. Too old to wield pick and shovel. Instead, each day I walk down by the shore and remember times before. I make up lines of verse to remember them. Every day, they are there beside me, still walking, still talking.

> *Genys a veuma in Kernow wheg,*
> *powyow kepar yw tanow;*
> *Me a dantas inhy mowes teg,*
> *Ann Tremellan o hy hanow*

And up in heaven, so as I believed, Cornish was spoken past the gates of St Peter.

'Ann Tremellan' was traditionally sung by an itinerant balladeer by the name of 'Uncle' Anthony James. James originated from Cury on the Lizard. He was a blind, ex-soldier who travelled much in West Cornwall. The surviving version of 'Ann Tremellan' is a composite. Only the first four lines of James' version exist, and these were recorded by the folklorist Robert Hunt in 1865. The rest of the verses are said to be a Cornish version of 'Barbara Allen', though these are purported to have been put in the style of James. The full ballad is contained in Ralph Dunstan's 1929 collection, The Cornish Song Book/Lyver Canow Kernewek.

10

The Pirate's Lament, or a Wild and Reckless Life

A Retelling of the Ballad 'The Flying Cloud' by Eric Maddern

For we sacked and plundered many a ship down upon the Spanish Main,
Caused many a widow and orphan in sorrow to remain.
To the crews we gave no quarter but gave them watery graves,
For the saying of our captain was: 'Dead men will tell no tales.'

ANON, Ireland

The pub outside Cork was known locally as 'Hitler's'. Its real name was 'Healey's' but the guy who used to run it had a Hitler-type mous-tache. That's Irish humour, I was told. We were there on a Sunday night, cards night. Friday night was story night, Saturday night, music night. We'd missed all that so resigned ourselves to an evening with Irish hurling on the TV and cards on the table. But one of the guys had been too drunk the night before to take his guitar home. So when the hurling finished someone asked him to get it out. After a couple of songs my local friend urged me to sing, which I duly did. And so the guitar did the rounds and more songs were sung.

Not long before midnight, it came back to me. I thought of the lovely 'Connemara Cradle Song' as an end-of-evening lullaby. Then I remembered something else, a ballad that starts in Waterford, just along the coast from Cork. It had to be that one. As an unaccompanied song I knew I'd to give it full power.

A couple of verses in and a few younger lads began to snigger. But some older men quickly hushed them. It seemed the entire pub was listening. More than halfway through I came to a line some seemed to know. They joined in: 'dead men tell no tales'. When I finally completed the thirteenth verse the room erupted. I had a standing ovation and men were leaning in to shake my hand. When we were leaving the pub a broad man by the door stopped me. 'That was alright,' he said, 'But I'll tell you something. I've never before seen the card game stop!'

So, what was the song? And how did I come to be singing it? And why might it have been useful to know in the lumber camps of Canada?

On my father's side of the family there's a tradition that five generations ago, in the 1830s, a Cornishman named John Maddern was the captain of a vessel apprehending pirates and slavers off the coast of Africa. I've long been intrigued by my great-great-great-great grandfather and I've always loved to sing, so when I found 'The Ballad of the *Flying Cloud*', it seemed right for me to sing it for I could imagine that my ancestor had played a part in it.

My name is William Hollander. I was born in the county of Waterford in 1805. As a boy I spent hours by the sea. I loved the sound of the waves churning the small stones on the beach. Later I'd go to the port, watch the ships and listen to tales of the old salts sitting on barrels by the water's edge. But I was my parents' only son and they wanted to be sure I had a proper trade. So I was apprenticed to a cooper by the name of William Brown. I served my master faithfully for eighteen months, learning to make casks, barrels and buckets by cutting, bending and binding wooden staves. During that time I fell in with the lovely Molly MacColl and promised her we'd be wed. But I was often down on the docks with the wares of my trade, and the lure of the sea was strong.

Finally my chance came. One day I was on the dockside admiring the *Ocean Queen* when I learned she was leaving on the next tide and needed a deck hand. It was a spur-of-the-moment decision. I packed my bag, said my swift farewells and, before anyone could change my mind, I was away, breathing deep the sea air, feeling the swell beneath my feet, off on a great adventure. I was filled with excitement like any seventeen-year-old on the threshold of his life's dream.

By the time we got to Bermuda's Isle I'd learned my way around the ship and up and down the rigging. I was a natural seaman and the world was my oyster. I was ready to go anywhere. But when I met with Captain Moore I stopped in my tracks. He was a big, broad man with black hair, a dark complexion and flashing eyes. A long jagged scar slashed across one side of his face. He scared me. But I looked him in the eye and when he asked me to join him on a slaving voyage to Africa aboard his ship, the *Flying Cloud*, promising me gold and high adventure, I couldn't say no. I was in his thrall. There was something powerful and ruthless about this man that drew me to him. I knew it was dangerous but I was young and bold and felt I would live forever.

So I left the *Ocean Queen* and joined the crew of the *Flying Cloud*. At first it was exhilarating. Captain Moore took a liking to me. He gave me varied work and I learned fast. Sometimes he'd reward me with extra rum and soon I was becoming one of the men, quick with a cheeky reply, always able to scamper up the rigging faster than anyone else. At that time I delighted in my life at sea. I even became good at the card games we played at night. Then we came to Africa's shore.

I thought I knew what it meant to be transporting slaves across the sea, but when I saw it close up something inside of me died – my youthful innocence perhaps. I saw men and women, cowed and beaten, marched onto the ship in chains. They were taken below and forced into dark, crowded, filthy conditions. Each one had scarcely eighteen inches to sit or lie in squalor. Sometimes one of them would look at me, a pleading look in the eye. I felt a pang of guilt, a desire to help. I knew they were human beings like me but there was nothing

I could do and so I turned away. My heart hardened. After a few days at sea the captives began dying of plague and fever. I was one of those who carried their bodies up on deck and threw them in the sea. It was sickening work and my mood changed. Gone was the exhilaration of my early days on board this ship. Now I was treating people like animals and I became animal-like myself. I didn't care any more. No more sympathy, no more fellow feeling. Just get on with the job. The temper of the weather seemed to reflect this change too. All across the Atlantic Ocean the winds blew and storms raged. It was a bitter time. I was relieved when we finally made it to the island of Cuba. There we shoved the surviving slaves ashore and sold them to the planters. At that moment I had another twinge of pity, knowing they'd have wretched lives tending rice, coffee and sugarcane beneath the baking sun. But when Captain Moore shared out the spoils I drowned my sorrows in rum and obliterated my remaining feelings of guilt.

We lived it up for a few weeks in Cuba. They were the glory days. We had money to spend and spend it we did. By now I'd passed my eighteenth birthday and really was one of the men. Sometimes fist-fights erupted over the card games and I found that, a couple of black eyes notwithstanding, I could hold my own. And I could drink with the best of them too. More than once I passed out in the arms of some devil woman I was sating my raw lust with in return for the clink of a few coins. But finally our money was all spent and it was time to go to sea again.

No one was keen to embark on another slaving trip. I certainly didn't want to go through that ordeal again.

Then it was that Captain Moore suggested something different, something that sent a thrill of terror and excitement through me. We would hoist the pirate flag aloft and scour the Spanish Main. That was the way to gold and silver, he said.

By now my moral compass was hopelessly adrift. So I cheered along with the rest of them at the thought of sailing under the skull and crossbones. There were only three of our entire crew who said 'no'. Two of them were Boston boys; the third was a lumberjack from Newfoundland. He'd become a friend and I was sorry to see him go. When these three dared to step back from the captain's plan, some of the younger lads sniggered and jeered. To my surprise Captain Moore said to leave them alone. If they wanted to stay ashore it was their choice. Now I wish to God I'd had the courage to go with them rather than stay with the captain. But by then I was used to living recklessly and had a taste for easy riches. I didn't yet know what piracy would mean, but I soon found out.

The *Flying Cloud* was a topsail schooner from Baltimore. She was one of the fastest ships that ever crested the waves so we never had trouble overtaking our quarry. As soon as we got a ship's crew in our power a short consultation was held and, if the majority felt it would be better to take life than to spare it, a single nod from our captain was sufficient. Regardless of age or sex, all entreaties for mercy were then in vain. In our intoxicated state we were untouched by the shrieks and groans of our victims. Rather there was competition between us to see who, with his own hands, could dispatch the greatest number in the shortest time. It was grim work.

Oh, God forgive me! How had I so quickly made the transition from virtuous youth to heartless, cut-throat murderer? Rarely did anyone escape our clutches alive. Some we forced to walk the plank.

Sometimes we set a few off in a small boat, but without any means of survival. When we'd plundered all valuables from the ship it was set on fire, the dying victims being consumed in the flames. How many widows and orphans we made I know not. But the captain's words rang in our ears: 'dead men tell no tales'. At least there would be no one left alive to betray us before a judge.

The months stretched into years and we continued to rule the waves, getting away with our shameful deeds. Most of the time we confined ourselves to our old cruising ground, intercepting vessels bound to and from Cuba. After plundering a ship we'd retreat to a small island to count our treasures and drink rum. Not surprisingly, arguments often broke out.

We had considerable success until the summer of 1830. Then we conceived a plan to head to the Azores and thence to Spain, where we'd divide the spoils, go ashore, separate and each one seek a new life. But by then word about the *Flying Cloud* had reached the British government. Before we could implement our plan we were being chased by frigates and liners. At first we shook them off like flies. But one day a British man o' war, the *Dungeness*, appeared over the horizon. This time we were not so lucky. Despite a full spread of sails we could not pull away. Instead the man o' war edged ever closer until at last she fired a shot across our bows. We still sped ahead but then a chain shot hit our main mast and brought it crashing to the deck. Now we had no choice but to fight for our lives.

It hadn't been long since we were laughing at the shrieks and groans of dying men and women, making fun of their agonised gestures. We weren't laughing now. We were fighting to the death. We fought with courage and skill, now thrusting, now dodging, mad as demons on an anvil. We did not give up, even though we were outnumbered, even though our comrades were slaughtered all around us. The deck ran deep with crimson blood. Our swords and daggers flashed on until suddenly there was a loud explosion amidships and our vessel was ablaze.

By then Captain Moore and thirty of our men were slain.

Somehow, amid all that savagery, I survived. Would that I had not. For as soon as my weapons were snatched from me I was bound like a slave, bundled into the hold and sent, with my fellows, for trial in London Town; to Newgate, where I am now, writing this …

I have been found guilty. I could hardly plead innocent. There is no other sentence but death for sinking and plundering ships on the Spanish Main. And so tomorrow I will wake up for the last time.

This is my dying declaration: I say sorry for letting down my mother and father who loved me and wished me only well. Sorry to my darling Molly, whose hand I'll never squeeze again. Sorry to the poor African captives I helped to transport over the sea into slavery. Sorry to all the innocent victims of my pirate crew and me. God have mercy on me. Now, at the age of only twenty-five, I must die. I have seen so much death I am not afraid ... though I dread to think what horrible way they might execute me. I hope for the usual hanging. The last thing I will say is this: 'Young men, don't do what I have done. It felt free and exciting at the time. But I regret it now. Take my warning. Shun all piracy.'

And so I give up my life.

'I knew William Hollander. I was the lumberjack from Newfoundland aboard the *Flying Cloud*. I'm glad I didn't stick with Captain Moore and become a pirate. But I kept my ear to the ground about what happened to his ship. I'd liked the lad from Waterford so when I found out that he was hanged I wanted to remember him. I thought about his life and made it into a song, 'The Ballad of the *Flying Cloud*'. I started singing it in the lumberjack camps of Canada. It's popularity spread and soon it was being sung in lumber camps everywhere. Later I heard that being able to sing the whole song was a qualification for getting job as a lumberjack in the backwoods. I must have caught some fire in those verses!'

I learned this song from Louis Killen's recording on Blow the Man Down – A Collection of Sea Songs and Shanties, *released by Topic Records in 1993. There's a slightly different version recorded by Ewan MacColl. The song appears in* Shantymen and Shantyboys – Songs of the Sailor and Lumberman *by William Doerflinger, published in 1951, and was later included in* The Book of Ballads *by MacEdward Leach, published in 1967. Doerflinger suggests its composition was influenced by a pamphlet, 'The Dying Declaration of Nicholas*

Fernandez', the confession of a pirate on the eve of his execution. 'The Dying Declaration' vividly depicts the depravity pirates were often reduced to and was originally put out as a temperance tract. I have drawn on it in my story.

Although there is no record of the song earlier than the 1880s, the events it depicts took place in the 1820s and '30s when the New World was being opened up and colonised by migrants from Europe. Land and riches were taken from the indigenous peoples everywhere who were either massacred or forced into servitude. The merchants and plantation owners of Britain and Western Europe became wealthy on slave labour and huge profits from the production of coffee, sugar and rice. Piracy offered men who'd been press-ganged on the streets freedom from the harsh punishments meted out on navy ships. There was an egalitarian spirit aboard pirate ships. So the captain was elected from the crew as the most skilled sailor and the bravest in combat. Spoils were divided up fairly according to agreed proportions. There was even a form of health insurance against injury received in the course of duty. So even though pirates could be very bloodthirsty, their thirst for liberty led them to cultivating some of the most democratic practices of their time. ('The Flying Cloud', Roud 1802/ Laws K28/G/D 1:44.)

11

The Shop Girl
and the Carpenter

A Retelling of the Ballad 'The Bristol Bridegroom or,
The Ship Carpenter's Love to a Merchant's Daughter'
by Laura Kinnear

In Bristol Town, as I have heard tell,
A rich merchant there did dwell.
He had a daughter beautiful and bright,
On her he fixed his own hearts delight

ANON, West Country

Polly Stagg, the daughter of Cuthbert Stagg of White & Mantle Department Store in Bristol, wafted around her father's shop in the latest fashions. This was despite the fact that Bristol, like everywhere else in the country, had endured clothes rationing for nearly a year. Cuthbert Stagg knew his daughter loved fashion and deliberately held back the most stylish utility wear for her coupons. He would also present her with yards of fabric, which Polly nimbly stitched into outfits equal to Worth or Lanvin. She would saunter through the linen department of which she was the manageress, in smart, tailored dresses, everyone's eyes on the generous swish of the fabric.

Cuthbert Stagg idolised his daughter – his only child – and since his wife had died five years ago when Polly was only fourteen, he had indulged her even more. There were only two things in Cuthbert Stagg's life: Polly and White & Mantle.

White & Mantle had survived the Bristol Blitz the previous year. In fact, the Blitz had been good for business as its main rival, Bonting's on Wine Street, had been battered and burnt by the Luftwaffe. Before the Blitz, White & Mantle had been in the unfashionable part of Bristol and had suffered from its dusty reputation, something Polly had tried to rectify by ordering more modern fancy goods. However, Cuthbert Stagg was an Edwardian man, his shop a relic of the late-Victorian age when his own father had first opened it. Nevertheless, with the destruction of Bonting's he now found himself swamped with customers, eagerly clutching their pink coupon books.

Polly had managed the linen department since she was sixteen years old; now nineteen, she possessed an enviable knowledge of her products, knowing her coloured brise brise from her Madras muslins, her Scotch lace from her Nottingham lace.

One day in late May, when Polly was folding a festooned Irish embroidered cotton sheet in the stock cupboard, a man dressed in overalls and carrying a small toolbox poked his head around the door.

'Excuse me Miss,' said the man who was around twenty, 'I've been told to fit some new shelves in your stock cupboard.'

Polly looked at the man who was tall like her, with pale blue eyes and bright blonde hair. Polly's eyes were drawn to the pencil that he had tucked on top of his ear. He noticed her looking at it and immediately whipped it away and held it awkwardly in his hand.

'I'm always losing pencils,' he said apologetically.

Polly was not used to seeing young men in White & Mantle, least of all in stock cupboards. She wondered why he wasn't away fighting like the rest of the men in Bristol.

'I'm on leave,' said the man, uneasily, as if he had read Polly's thoughts, 'I'm only back home for two weeks. I work for my father.'

'Me too,' said Polly, blushing, and she rolled her eyes and laughed, finding it difficult not to stare at him.

'I have to fetch the wood,' he said. 'I'll be back in a moment.'

Polly nodded and she could feel her cheeks flame. When he walked out of the stock cupboard Polly gently closed the door and then rested her body against the wall, feeling it tingle and pulse. Who was this young carpenter who had just abruptly wandered into her life? Five minutes ago she was organising bed sheets, now everything had changed.

A few minutes later there was a knock at the stock cupboard door.

'Polly!' said a man firmly.

Polly knew that voice – it was Mr Webb from Glassware. She opened the door to see him and the young man carrying two planks of wood in their hands.

'Let us in then,' said Mr Webb, busily, bustling in front of her, 'young Aleksy has a job to get on with.'

So his name is Aleksy thought Polly to herself, how unusual, and she conjured up a fascinating and tragic story about how he was the son of Russian spies.

'I'll leave you to it then,' said Mr Webb and he nodded, somewhat deferentially, to Polly.

Nothing more was seen or heard of Polly and Aleksy that morning. It took Aleksy nearly three hours to put up two shelves, although everyone did say he had done a beautiful job when they stood back to admire them. They also complimented Polly on the organisation of the linens, which were folded exquisitely on the shelves in crisp, neat bundles.

At lunchtime Polly gave a vague, stammering excuse to her father about popping out for a bottle of cod liver oil from Larcher's, the chemist.

However, instead of going to Larcher's, Polly went to meet Aleksy by the old castle. It was a neglected spot since the Blitz, with many of the buildings sad, tattered ruins. When Polly saw Aleksy walking towards her she ran and then they quickly kissed, like they had done in the stock cupboard only an hour before. Then they grasped each other's hands and began chattering about their lives, Aleksy's proving to be as romantic as Polly had imagined. He told her he'd been born in Bristol, but his parents were refugees from the Revolution. He described how his father had made a living from carpentry and had also taught him the skills to fashion and carve in wood. Polly looked at her watch: an hour had passed and she still hadn't fetched the cod liver oil.

'Meet me tonight,' said Aleksy. 'Come to my house and my mother will cook dinner.'

Polly promised she would but a gnawing in her stomach told her that her father wouldn't approve of Aleksy.

Polly and her father arrived back home at six o'clock that evening after White & Mantle had closed. They lived in a narrow Regency house which hadn't been decorated since Cuthbert's parents had moved there as a newly married couple in the 1880s. The walls were pasted with anaglypta and, as Cuthbert preferred to keep the heavy velvet curtains closed at all times to prevent the fade of the fabrics, artificial light was required even in the height of summer. Despite White & Mantle having installed electric lighting twenty years ago, Cuthbert was determined to live by gas lamps and candles in his own home.

That evening, father and daughter sat in the sitting room on uncomfortable saddleback chairs and drank weak tea out of Polly's grandmother's silver teapot, the flickering light of the gas lamp reflecting on its mirror-like surface.

'I'm going out tonight,' said Polly nervously, thinking it better to blurt it out, rather than skirting round the issue.

'Tonight? Why?' said Cuthbert, resting his teacup on the saucer with a chink.

'I've been asked to dinner,' said Polly, 'by a young man called Aleksy.'

Polly watched as her father's skin changed from the colour of parchment to the colour of poppies.

'I knew I shouldn't have employed that Bolshevik,' said her father. 'You're not going to dinner with communists! You will go up to your room at once and I will hear no more about it.'

Polly let out a heartbroken gasp and then a loud sniff as she rushed from the sitting room and up to her bedroom on the second floor. She slammed the door and then let herself fall into a hot, panting temper onto the floorboards. She simply must get to Aleksy's somehow she sobbed to herself; she didn't care what her father said anymore.

Fortunately for Polly, her bedroom window had access to a very sturdy cast-iron downpipe. After the difficult task of securing her sash window with its snapped cord, she easily manoeuvred herself onto the pipe, finally hitting the stone slabs in the yard in her best snakeskin shoes. She then furtively opened the back gate and ran all the way to the Docks, where Aleksy lived.

Aleksy's house was a cramped, weatherboard cottage on the edge of the river. When Aleksy answered the door he appeared even more handsome than she remembered, with his blonde hair combed and his blue eyes shining with excitement. He kissed her on the cheek, and then led her into the small kitchen-cum-sitting room where she was met by his father, mother and two sisters, all of whom had the same blonde hair and blue eyes as Aleksy. Aleksy's father fetched a chair for her to sit on next to the range, which was crammed with bubbling pans ready for dinner.

Polly looked around and examined the objects in Aleksy's home: the stack of books with Cyrillic letters on the spines, the handmade wooden boxes, the porcelain plate with its view of a white and gold fairytale castle. Polly also noticed the fine lace curtains, letting in a stream of warm, yellow evening light.

'Did you make the curtains?' said Polly to Aleksy's mother, a small woman who was now stood at the range stirring a thick, purple soup.

'Yes', she replied, 'I make all my things, even the clothes I am wearing,' and she laughed and gestured towards the sewing machine in the corner.

'They're beautiful,' said Polly, 'better than anything we sell in White & Mantle.'

Aleksy's mother smiled broadly and began ladling the soup into bowls, passing the first one to Polly.

After dinner Aleksy walked Polly back home through the moonlit city streets. They walked hand in hand, although both were silent. As they reached the corner of Polly's road, she quickly pulled away and said in a panic, 'My father can't see us. I disobeyed him tonight by coming to your house.'

Polly watched Aleksy as he bowed his head in the milky light of the moon. 'I've not been honest with you this evening either,' he said, avoiding her eyes. 'I received a telegram this afternoon informing me I must return to my base at Portsmouth. We're to embark on a secret mission.'

'When do you have to leave?' said Polly, her voice wavering.

'Tomorrow.'

'Then we still have tonight,' said Polly and she grabbed Aleksy by the hand and they walked away together back into the blackout.

The following morning Polly turned up for work with her skirt suit crumpled and her make-up smudged. Cuthbert Stagg, a naive, trusting man, had never thought to check her bedroom and therefore her disappearance had gone unnoticed. When Polly asked to leave work early because of a headache, her father agreed without question, convinced by her uncharacteristically dishevelled appearance that his daughter was truly unwell.

Instead of going home Polly walked the other way towards the Docks with several yards of navy blue fabric in her carpetbag. When she arrived at Aleksy's house he had already left for Portsmouth but his mother let her in with a conspiratorial nod and led her immediately to the sewing machine. Five hours later Polly was hurtling towards Portsmouth in a crammed railway carriage, her hair shorn and her slender body swamped by a finely stitched copy of a British Naval Uniform.

When Polly reached Portsmouth harbour it was past midnight and the clear skies of the previous night had been replaced by thick cloud. However, she had no trouble in finding Aleksy's ship, the HMS *Viola*. She found herself becoming part of the buzz of the embarking officers, who in their swarm led her to the great, grey ship sat on the dull, metallic sea, like a giant, majestic seal. Polly stared at the guns, which looked to her like outstretched arms, spoiling for a fight. The comforting smells of White & Mantle – face compact powder mingled with fox fur – had been replaced by oil and jute and for a few moments Polly doubted her courage, and fingered the

collar of her uniform with apprehension. Then she recalled Aleksy's corn-coloured hair and, with a determined sigh, she plucked a packet of cigarettes from her pocket, thrust one between her lips and lit it with a shaking match. Polly let the cigarette hang in her mouth like she'd seen men do – young men who came into White & Mantle to buy their sweethearts artificial silk stockings.

At first Polly couldn't find a safe way onto the ship, as the main gangplank was thronged with high-ranking officers rifling through papers. Finally she noticed an opening at the side, which was half door, half hatch, and after checking that there was no one else around she slipped straight through it. As soon as she landed inside she was met with a voice that said with unconcealed amusement, 'Prefer the tradesman's entrance?'

Polly tried not to look startled as she realised that she'd landed into a private cabin, and moreover one which was stacked with boxes and tins of medical supplies.

'I'm the doctor's assistant,' she said hastily to the man stood in front of her, as she caught sight of a set of syringes. 'They told me to come straight to you.'

At first the man seemed puzzled and he asked Polly for her ID card and papers. Polly reached into her pocket and pulled out the documents that Aleksy's parents had so expertly faked. Despite their artistry, Polly could feel her ears pound as the man carefully examined them, the ink barely dry on the blue card. To Polly's relief the man handed them back to her with a smile and said, 'They're always threatening to give me more help, typical that they should send you here without warning.'

Polly gave a dismissive shrug and in her best gravelly voice said, 'That's management for you.'

'Yes, it is rather,' said the man and he held out his hand for Polly to shake and said, 'John Peacock, Surgeon Lieutenant of the HMS *Viola*, very pleased to meet you.' Then, as he let go of Polly's hand, he said thoughtfully, 'I shouldn't wonder that you've been chosen as a doctor's mate. You've been blessed with the nimblest, slenderest hands I've ever seen on a man.'

That night, after learning from John that the ship was bound for Normandy, Polly wandered alone onto the deck and imagined the French coast appearing before her in the darkness. John had also told her that the ship was to be part of a raid that would begin in the early hours of the morning, just before sunrise. The men were to attack the port of Dieppe with the aim of holding it to gain intelligence. As an assistant to the Surgeon Lieutenant, Polly was not part of the planned invading force.

'We'll need you,' John had said gravely as he explained the plans for attack, 'I've my doubts about this mission.'

At 5 a.m. exactly the HMS *Viola* arrived at Dieppe and launched its landing force. A stream of vessels embarked, crowded with helmeted men, their guns clasped to their chests.

Polly watched the men leave, her eyes desperately seeking Aleksy's fair head.

Then, suddenly she saw him as he stumbled aboard a small craft, his eyes briefly glancing at her as he turned his back to the ship. Polly bit her lip hard to halt her tears, and the sharp pain gave her a strange sense of comfort and relief.

Five hours later and the sea was red with men's blood. Landing craft lay abandoned on the beach like discarded bones and Polly shook in horror as she cleaned and bandaged. She recalled with grim irony that four days ago she'd recoiled from sticking a plaster on the finger of Millie Forbes in Glassware, after she'd smashed a stem vase. Polly suddenly felt that her life before this moment had been a pathetic, trifling thing. She desperately searched the features of the wounded men for the face of Aleksy, recalling with heartbreak the last, indifferent look he had inadvertently given her.

By 10.50 a.m. the Allies had retreated and the HMS *Viola* skulked away, its crew reduced to 400 men, groaning in the summer morning sunshine. Some still lay in the landing craft, now stationed back on ship, awaiting the surgeon's attention. The last man to be seen had hair drenched with thick, sticky blood, which obliterated its natural colour.

'This one's got a nasty head wound,' said John, as they lifted the man onto a makeshift bed, 'he'll need some of your expert stitching.' Polly washed the man's face, the water turning pink as she sponged the deep gash by his ear. She revealed bloodied eyes and a nose shredded at the corners, a face changed, but still recognisable as that of Aleksy.

'Aleksy, Aleksy, my love,' she whispered as she doused his head in iodine. She then licked a long piece of thread, pushed it through a needle and began to make small stitches in his splitting skin. Aleksy howled then and it took all her resolve to not reveal herself to him.

When HMS *Viola* returned to Portsmouth in the early evening Aleksy was asleep. Looking at his face, bruised, yet so peaceful after the pain of the stitching, Polly could not resist placing a kiss on his lips. As she did so she noticed someone behind her and she sprung up.

'Excuse me officer,' said John sternly, 'I don't believe its medical practice to embrace the wounded.' At this moment Aleksy also opened his eyes and they rested on Polly with confusion.

Polly opened her mouth to offer an excuse, but instead she grabbed Aleksy's hand and with all pretence gone wailed, 'I'm no officer, just a Bristol shop girl who followed her sweetheart aboard ship!'

Aleksy, stiff from his wounds, winced as he sat up in his bed and said in a hoarse voice, 'You did that for me?'

Polly nodded, tears now crammed in her eyes.

'You're mad … you could have died!' said Aleksy.

'*You* could have died,' said Polly.

'Well we'll have to marry now,' said Aleksy and he grinned, laying his head back on his pillow, Polly's hand still firmly in his.

Polly and Aleksy were married the following day in Portsmouth, he in his naval uniform, she in crepe de chine. Polly was forever thankful that Portsmouth was home to Lacy's, a department store not unlike White & Mantle with an enviable range of ready-to-wear.

THE SHOP GIRL AND THE CARPENTER

This story is based on the ballad 'The Bristol Bridegroom Or, The Ship Carpenter's Love to a Merchant's Daughter' (Roud V29410). It dates from the seventeenth century and broadsides survive from the eighteenth century, now held at The Bodleian Libraries, amongst others. The mention of the storming of Dieppe gave me the idea of setting it in the Second World War. Its original Bristol setting seemed to segue perfectly into a post-Blitz Bristol, as did the idea of a wealthy seventeenth-century merchant becoming a department store owner. Similarly the determined cross-dressing maiden of the original ballad needed only a few tweaks to turn her into the impulsive Polly.

12

A Testament of Love

A Retelling of the Ballad 'Sovay'
by Karola Renard

Sovay, Sovay, all on one day,
She drest herself in man's array,
With a brace of pistols hanging by her side,
To meet her true love and away did ride.

ANON

The star shell pierced the darkness without sound. Sophie gazed at it in wonder as it illuminated the sky with its geyser of light.

Then a bullet hit the bonnet of her ambulance.

Sophie's heart skipped a beat. She killed the engine and scrambled out of the seat, cursing as her bulky greatcoat caught on the stepping board. On her stomach, she crawled into the cover of some splintered trees. There she lay still, but could feel her body tremble with shock. To her right, she sensed the drop of a shell crater. She was close to the German trenches and had been on her way to pick up wounded men from the frontline. Now she was stuck.

A stray sniper bullet, she tried to reassure herself. This was an ambulance, for Christ's sake! Not that this meant you could not get killed. Sophie had come a long way from the salons of Mayfair in learning that in this war you had better not take chances.

She pulled up her kerchief to protect her nose from the foul smell that rose from the crater. Sophie always drove like this, kerchief

hiding her face and hat pulled down firmly over her eyes to keep off dust, rain or snow. The other girls in her unit had followed her example and it had earned them the nickname 'The Highwaymen Corps'. It suited her. Everything was better than being Lady Sophia Dennison, choking on her silver spoon.

The initial shock subsided and Sophie began to feel restless. The fighting had been heavy and there were hundreds of men waiting, with only a handful of ambulances available. She craned her neck to get a better view of her vehicle and the road that lay once more in starless obscurity. There had been no more shells, so the Hun would not be able to see her from the trenches. But if a sniper was close, he would detect her movement. Sophie cursed, using language she did not even know existed until coming to France. Heart pounding rapidly, she began to slowly edge out of the thicket, eyes fixed on the road.

Then she saw the ring.

It lay on a stack of rotten leaves as if presented to her as a gift. Sophie had just closed her hand around it when her leg lost touch with the ground and kicked mud into the crater. There was a splash and, deep down, a moan.

Sophie froze, listening hard.

Nothing. Had she imagined it?

She took a deep breath and slowly got to her feet.

And then she ran.

It was dawn when Sophie stumbled into her billet and fell on the bed fully clothed, too exhausted to take off her boots.

Only in the evening, when she sat alone by the stove did she recall last night's strange find. Out of her tunic pocket came the ring and lay before her on the table. It was a simple golden band, the only ornament an inscription on the inside.

Sophie held it close to her face. '*Du hast meiner Liebe Pfand*', she read. 'You hold the Pledge of my Love.' Sophie had always been good at German, a fact she wished she had kept from her superiors who, whenever necessary, despatched her to perform small favours for the wounded Germans – writing letters, explaining about treatments and in turn translating their anxious questions regarding an uncertain future as prisoners of war. It was a task Sophie loathed wholeheartedly.

Still holding the ring, her gaze fell on a stack of mostly unopened letters. Her fiancé, Graham, worked for the War Office and was completely at ease with himself, his life and the war – apart from the fact that Sophie was in it. He hated the idea that his pretty intended was spoiled by the base, albeit necessary, business of war. But Sophie had not given in to his insistence and had postponed their wedding 'for the duration of the war'. But unlike so many, Sophie felt like she had signed up for life, not death. Joining the Ambulance Corps had given her a freedom she had never known before – she had not only learned to drive but had, within weeks, become an accomplished engineer. She would have been happy, had it not been for her brothers.

Their death was grinding inside her, scraping her raw from the inside out as if she was a lifeless, flaccid hide, not a human being. It was a piercing, edgy pain and it never went away. Since Daniel's death, eight month ago, she had numbed the pain by keeping busy. But then, a few days ago, another telegram had arrived informing her that Toby, too, had been lost. The tension had been building ever since. Her skin prickled and itched with it and she had started to scratch herself bloody at night.

Whenever she thought of her three brothers, a macabre counting rhyme she had heard soldiers sing started to go round and round in her head as if stuck on a loop:

Three little soldier boys left home and said adieu,
one stepped on a blind shell, and then there were two.
Two little soldier boys went over the top at dawn,
one walked into machine-gun fire and then there was only one.

Only one left. Her youngest brother was in England, recuperating from a facial wound. None of it felt real. In her mind, Daniel and Toby remained alive. She still expected to receive their letters, still thought of them as 'out there', and sometimes she seemed to spot their dear familiar faces amongst the waves of wounded that flooded in day after day like a bilious tide.

She had never mentioned this to Graham, as she knew what he would say: 'King and country and a glorious cause'. It was what people said who had never been at the front. Absentmindedly, she twisted the ring in her fingers. What should she do with it? Was its owner still alive?

Suddenly, a hot rage shot through her and she flung the ring across the room where it landed on the wooden planks with an irritating 'plink'.

She remembered the ashen face of Toby's wife as she stared at his kitbag that had been returned to her, the smell of gas and filthy water slowly creeping through the room. She remembered Daniel's fiancé, wailing open-mouthed like an abandoned baby. Somewhere in Germany, a woman might still look onto the ring's counterpart with longing and hope. The thought filled Sophie with nauseous despair. She would throw it away. On her next drive, she would fling it far into no man's land, and this unknown woman's hope would stretch in vain, drowning in the same yellow mud that had killed her brothers.

A VAD stuck her head through the door. 'You are needed Soph. On the main ward.'

'Never heard of knocking?' Sophie snapped and the other girl hastily withdrew. Stiffly, Sophie stood up and picked up the ring, threading it onto the chain round her neck that made her the dutiful wearer of Graham's engagement ring. She slipped both rings under her kerchief where their reluctant union would be hidden from view.

'Here he is', one of the orderlies said, pointing to a bed in the corner. 'Found him in a shell crater, apparently. He's in a bad way, but he just won't stop talking. Blethering on about someone called Hilda, I think. Don't know much German, do I?'

'And what should I do with him?' Sophie asked, hostile. The orderly shrugged.

'Talk to him.' When he saw the expression on her face, he added, 'Have some heart, girl. The chap's dying.'

'So are many. I'm sure he's killed his fair share.'

The man shook his head sadly and turned away. Over his shoulder he said, 'Order from above, so you better get on with it.'

Sophie ran a hand through her cropped hair – another thing she hadn't told Graham about – and forced her feet into the direction of the bed where the German soldier tossed and turned.

She pulled her breeches up and sat on the stool beside the bed, looking down on to her charge. He was tall, long legs twitching under the covers. Blonde hair fell over his forehead, hiding his eyes. His lips were in constant motion, forming a stream of words Sophie could not make out. Every now and then he groaned.

Sophie did not move. She just sat very still and felt hate oozing out of her like black bile. Her mind was like a merry-go-round, turning the same thought over and over again: *someone like you killed my brothers*. There was a space inside her filled with condensed darkness, like poison gas pressed into the hollow that Daniel and Toby had left behind. It made her feel breathless with loathing.

Still, she could not take her eyes of him.

His hands slid restlessly over the covers. He raised his voice in anguish and all of a sudden said clearly in German, 'I've lost the ring, Hilda. I'm so sorry.'

Sophie went cold.

And then it all fell into place.

A shell crater, they had said. Suddenly, she was there again, looking at the ring on its bed of leaves, hearing a groan in the darkness. Her hand shot up to her neck where the ring sat, and it was to her as if she could feel it twitch, anxious to be reunited with its owner. Sophie's heart began to beat faster and the darkness in her grew more solid.

The German kept muttering, talking to his absent lover with a feverish anguish that wove around Sophie like a drug. Her head pounded and she pressed her hands against her temples, but the pain increased. Images flared up: strange, unconnected fragments that pierced the protective veil of her mind ...

Black rain over no man's land, falling onto corpses half-buried in the mud by retreating troops. Dead children in the streets of a town in which no wall was higher than Sophie's knees. A man with shrapnel splinters in his eyes, blindly weeping blood. Men with no faces, holes gaping where their noses should be. Men strung on barbed wire like beads, one body linked with the next like petals in a perverse daisy chain ...

Sophie thumbed her forehead to drive the memories back, but it was no use. The throbbing in her head was winding up to a sharp crescendo.

All the while, the bloody German was still talking, on and on it went this intense evocation of love and yearning. *Shut up*, Sophie thought. *Shut up. Shut up.* But he kept speaking to the empty air, his voice reaching out to a different time, a different world. The merry-go-round in Sophie's head was spinning so fast now, it made her feel dizzy. *You killed my brothers. You killed my brothers ...*

On the bed next to the German she noticed stacks of unused bedding. Slowly, Sophie got to her feet and took a pillow from the pile, cradling it in her arm like a lover. Then she bent over the German and looked down on the body on the sweat-soaked covers. His breathing was shallow, the movement of his chest under the bloody bandage hardly noticeable.

Sophie lowered the pillow.

Suddenly the German sat up and stared at her.

'Hilda?' he asked hoarsely.

The pillow fell to the ground and the moment of madness was over.

His eyes were blue and stared at her in wonder. It reminded her of the way Toby had looked at her when they were children and she had played the piano or done something else he was impressed with. She would never forget that look of innocent wonder.

Her hands began to shake. She hugged herself, trying to stop the violent tremor that had gripped her body. Horrified at what she had been about to do, she looked at the man's face and saw pure love.

'Hilda,' he said, staring past her into the distance. 'It's ... you. I did ... not think ...'

Without thinking, she took the young man's hand and eased him back onto the pillows.

'Yes,' she heard her own voice say soothingly. 'It's Hilda. I'm here.'

Another voice, alone in the silence of her head, raged and screamed. *What are you doing?* She didn't know. All she knew was that he was looking at her with Toby's eyes.

He closed his eyes and lay back, exhausted, but with a smile tugging at his lips. Then he seemed to remember something distressing, and his features became anxious. 'Hilda', he whispered. 'I lost the ring Hilda.'

'What ring?' she asked him, feeling it burn on her collarbone.

He tried to clear his throat, his eyes pleading with her.

'The ring ... I ... made for you. In your ... workshop ... one day. You ... laughed ... I was ... clumsy. You ... so ... good with your ... hands, Hilda ... but I ... I made it ... for you.'

Like from afar, Sophie heard herself say in German, 'And you put all your love into it.'

He laughed a little and his laugh turned into a cough that racked his lean body. When he had calmed down, he said, 'You ... teased me. But then ... you read ...'

'You hold the pledge of my love,' Sophie said.

He looked at her without really seeing her, eyes shining with the love she had invoked. Again, he reached for her. She gave him her hand.

'I ... I went ... down on ... on ...'

'You asked me to marry you.'

His fingers reached up blindly, searching for her face.

'You cut ... your hair ... said ... you would ... never ... liked ... doing things like ...'

'Like everyone else?'

He smiled up at her, caressing her with his gaze. He had a sweet smile, Sophie thought, a smile that bathed you in a warm glow. How Hilda must miss that smile.

'And what did I say?' she asked him. 'When you asked me to marry you?'

He was still smiling.

'... teasing me ...'

'I just want to hear it from you.'

'You ... you said ... Peter ... first ... I make you ... a ring ... but ...'

'But?'

'The war ...'

'So I gave you mine. To keep safe?'

'Yes ...'

'And I promised to marry you.'

His smile widened to a faint grin.

'You ... did ... though ... you never ... agree ... with me ...'

Sophie felt an involuntary smile spreading over her face.

'I'm sure that's not true.'

'It ... is.'

'Am I that stubborn?

'A ... mule. A ... lovely ... mule.'

'Oh. Thanks a lot.'

He closed his eyes in exhaustion, still smiling, holding onto her hand.

'I think ... about you ... all ... the time. Stay ... the same ... for me ... don't change ... if I don't ... come back ...'

'Don't say that.'

The cry had escaped her mouth, anguished, echoing over lands and borders, fallen from the lips of a rebellious young artist called Hilda who had nothing left of her love but the ring he had made her.

'Promise.'

'I will not let anything ever change me.'

'For ... me.'

'Promise.'

Sophie bend down and kissed him lightly on the forehead. He clung on to her hand and suddenly his eyes were glistening with tears.

'Lost … the ring … so … sorry.'

'Shh.' Sophie put a finger to his lips. 'No, Peter. It is here. Look.'

She hastily unfastened the necklace and showed him the ring, then gently took his hand and slipped it on his finger. His hands were long and slender like a woman's and it fitted perfectly. Sophie smiled.

Peter touched it, incredulous.

Sophie pushed him back onto the bed, gently but firmly.

'You need to sleep now.'

He didn't resist, resting his cheek on the hand with the ring.

'Stay?' he whispered.

'Yes, of course I will.'

When Sophie woke up in the morning, stiff and dazed, he was dead.

She found Hilda's address amongst the letters Peter had carried in his greatcoat pocket and slipped them into her tunic alongside the ring. It slid from his finger easily as if it knew it was time to return to its owner. Then she walked out of the ward and kept walking until she reached a patch of wood that had not yet been touched by the war.

There she sat down and howled with grief until her voice was raw and spent. She cried for her brothers and their loved ones, for Peter and Hilda, and for herself. She cried until the poisonous blackness was purged and her heart could breathe again.

That day, she wrote two letters and received one. She wrote to Graham and ended their engagement; and she wrote to Hilda, knowing that this letter had to be saved for a peace yet to come. And she got a letter from her mother: her youngest brother had been demobbed and returned home. For him, the war was over.

Before she went on her shift that evening, she visited Peter's hastily dug grave. One of the orderlies stood bent over the cross, and as he straightened and looked at her, Sophie saw that it bore no inscription.

'Must go and ask what his name was,' the orderly said, wiping his nose with his sleeve. 'Would not like any chap to be buried without a name.'

Sophie nodded. 'His name was Peter', she said. 'Peter Hart.'

'Doesn't sound German,' the man said, puzzled. 'With that name, he could have been one of ours.'

'Yes', Sophie said quietly, 'he could have been.'

For a moment, she stood in silence. Then she turned and climbed into the ambulance. She pulled up her kerchief and turned the key. With a fierce roar, the engine sprang into life.

This story is based on the ballad 'Sovay' (Sovay: Roud 7/Laws N21) in which a young woman dresses up as a highwayman to test her lover's commitment. In writing, I was inspired by women such as Vera Brittain, Dorothy Fielding, Elsie Knocker and Mairi Chisholm who found in the gruesome theatre of the First World War an opportunity for emancipation whilst the society they lived in was still largely ruled by the oppressive standards of Victorian morality.

❧ 13 ❧

'There Ain't No Sweet Man'

A Retelling of the Ballad 'The Famous Flower of Serving Men' by Kirsty Hartsiotis

A braver bower you never did see
Than my true-love did build for me.
But there came thieves late in the night,
They rob'd my bower, and slew my knight,
And after that my knight was slain,
I could no longer there remain.

ANON

That last evening became like a moment from a dream for Nell. It was nothing special. Jake was singing 'Painting the Clouds with Sunshine' to their son, who gurgled up at his daddy. She sipped her Southside. The windows were all flung open in the heat, moths were buzzing up against the mesh and she could hear the shushing of the sassafras trees. Bliss. Not that she knew it then. She remembered thinking that the baby would never get to sleep if Jake played him up like that. Her peach silk negligee was torn and she was annoyed that the servants had taken the weekend off. Still, after she'd put the kid down, she and Jake went to bed all smiles.

She woke in the middle of the night. Her eyes searched the blackness, but out there in the sticks there were no streetlights and neon signs to break the night. She heard a thump. Could've been anything, but it set her heart racing. Jake didn't stir. Was it footsteps? Had Jake's man come back early?

'Jake?' But he was fast asleep.

She was sure there was someone out there. Was that the creak of the parlour door opening? She turned on the light, clocked the time: 3:15 a.m. The door flew open. Through it burst a gang of men, all holding shotguns aimed straight at them.

She screamed.

The baby began to wail.

Jake bolted up beside her.

The men wore black, as if they'd peeled themselves out of the night. The man in front spoke, 'Remember, don't hurt the broad.'

Jake gave her a shove and she fell to the floor.

Then the air was alive with the terrible staccato pulse of the guns. A bullet hit the wall behind her. Worse, far worse, were the soft thuds that followed. Jake's screams. Spats of red splashed onto her negligee, her arms, her hair. The baby was wailing, she was screaming; but from the men there came no sound save the thunk, thunk, thunk of their guns.

When the guns stopped, the spokes-man grated, 'Get up.'

She obeyed, shaking, but nearly fell when she saw Jake spread-eagled on the bed. The white sheets soaked red. His staring eyes.

'W-why?' she cried. 'W-who?'

They said nothing, but a man turned towards the cot. In a heart-beat she understood and without thought she was at the cot, pulling the baby into her arms.

'No! No! You can't! Sir, that's my baby, please, don't, please.'

She clasped her son so tight that his cries increased, his body warm and squirming against her.

The man didn't look at her, just grabbed the baby.

'No! You'll have to kill me first – please, he's just a baby!'

The man was so much stronger, the silk of her negligee so slippery, and fear coated her hands with sweat. Her baby was torn from her, tossed on the bed and –

The guns beat again.

The baby's cries stopped.

After a long moment the spokesman said, 'Kid, I don't know what you did to hack off your mother, but you sure got on the wrong side of her. Don't think of calling the fuzz. You'll think you got off lucky tonight if you do.'

They trashed the house as they left.

It seemed as if hours had passed, but the clock said 3:45. Numb, seeking comfort where there was none, she crawled onto the bed and huddled against the bodies of her husband and child.

Nell never knew how she got them outside the next morning. She found a shovel, and, in the shade of a sassafras tree, dug a grave. She eased off Jake's ring and her baby's locket. Then she placed the baby in his father's arms and covered them with earth.

Only then did she weep. At length, she looked at her dirt-covered hands, at the blood that soaked her negligee, and something finally snapped.

Back to the house she ran. In a fever she stripped off the negligee. Ran a bath. Even when the blood was gone, still she scrubbed. She didn't recognise her face in the mirror. Her long blonde hair hung in straggles around a gaunt, blotchy face. Recoiling, she grabbed a pair of nail scissors and began to hack at her hair until it was all gone.

Back in the blood-soaked bedroom flies buzzed all around. She was so numb she hardly noticed. From the wardrobe she drew a shirt, trousers, a jacket. Jake's scent was still on them: laundry powder, cologne, a faint male muskiness.

She inhaled. Tears tracked her cheeks. Socks. His shoes wouldn't do, but there were her own brogues. A coat, despite the heat, and a trilby.

Back to the mirror. In place of the distraught woman was a thin boy with spiky yellow hair, dressed in slightly too-big clothes. A bitter smile quirked her face. Thank God she wasn't five foot two, with eyes of blue. She didn't even look like a masculine woman: rather, a feminine man.

She slipped Jake's ring onto her thumb, hid her baby's locket under her tie and then she was out of the house and walking as fast as she could into the night.

Morning found her in the city, sitting in a coffee shop. The scene played over and over in her mind – the men, the guns, the blood, the screaming – until she wanted to scream herself. But smartly dressed young men in downtown coffee shops don't scream.

She paced the streets until her legs ached. All around, the buildings soared in white stone, smooth contours, like huge machines thrusting their heads into the sky. The sun baked the sidewalks. She couldn't eat. She just walked, no destination, no thought.

As dusk approached, some native sense made her realise that she had to get shelter. The streets were emptying as people made their way home to their tea for two. She twisted Jake's ring, and allowed herself to think about what the man had said. How could her stepmother have done it? She hated Jake, yes. So her father had hidden her and Jake out in the sticks. But to kill an innocent baby? That wasn't the gangster way, was it? She wasn't safe. But where was? Her mouth quirked and moments later she was striding downtown.

A dead-end lane, one flickering neon sign for a Chinese laundry at the end. Dank, the smell of starch. Someone there ahead of her, trench-coated, hat downturned. A knock. The sudden flare of light and noise, the figure slipping inside and then darkness again. How many times had she and Jake come here for their bootleg hooch? She buttoned up her overcoat and pulled down her own hat. Knocked. Flashed her signet ring, and was gratified to see the man's eyes widen a little. Then she was in. Warmth and light pooled over her, and she walked towards the growing sound of music and laughter below.

At the top of the steps down she looked down into the bar. A curtained stage ringed with tables where a woman was singing. Dark-suited men with glad-rag dolls perched on their laps. The smell of sweat, cheap perfume and alcohol. And there, surrounded by cronies, the man who was going to protect her, even though he didn't know it yet – Tony Da Re, the boss of the family that ran this joint. Young. Slickly handsome. Toying with a glass of champagne. Someone whispered in his ear and his startled gaze lifted to take her in.

She was soon in front of him. Faced by his hard-eyed appraisal of her it was difficult to feel like a man. Surely they'd know?

'Whaddya want from the boss?' said a man. 'Flashing the Fiore ring an' all?'

Pitching her voice as low as she could, she tried out her story. 'I'm Bill – Guilliamo Fiore. They threw me out – put my fingers on someone's property. So, to hell with them, I say. I'm joining the Da Res!' She faltered. 'I mean, I know I did wrong. I need just one more chance ...'

The men looked at her, frowning. But Da Re himself was smiling. 'I do have a position going. My valet up and left with his broad the other day. Can you keep house? Press clothes? Mix a drink?'

She nodded, her heart racing. Of course she could. She was – *had been* – a wife, after all.

'Then I've got a flat where you can hang your hat. The position's yours.'

'Truly? You wouldn't fool me, would you?'

Da Re laughed. It lit up his face. 'No, kid. But this better be for real – you're a Fiore, after all. They're no friends of the Da Res.'

The men looked furious, but what could they do? He was the boss.

She became Da Re's valet. She lost herself in the work. Ironed his shirts. Aired his apartment. Mixed his drinks. Listened as he talked. Hours would go by and she wouldn't think about Jake and her son at all. Then it would all come rushing back. She locked it down and threw herself back into pleasing Tony.

Soon she knew all about him. He hid it well. She watched him chat up the flappers, but she saw how his eyes followed any pretty young man who entered the club. Saw how he looked at her – at *Bill*. Sometimes his hand would rest on her shoulder or pat her knee. She'd freeze. His eyes would darken with sorrow and he'd withdraw.

There was a restlessness in him. In all of them, those days. In the frenetic dancing, the drinking behind locked doors, in the lines of cocaine on the tables. Every night they went to the club. Men would come and go. She took to standing behind Tony. She had a better-fitting suit now. She'd bound down her breasts and was just a slim, black-clad figure with cropped yellow hair. It made the clients uncomfortable. Most of the time, Tony liked that.

That night, when the client was gone, he pulled her down to sit beside him.

'Enough with the glowering. Sheesh, you're so thin – don't you ever eat?'

She shrugged.

'Live a little, Billy.'

He was smiling. She saw his eyes flick around, and then his hand was on her knee. 'Tony, please ...'

His smile fell away.

'You never look at the girls, Billy. So ...'

She couldn't see her expression, but that darkness came into his eyes at whatever he saw. Before she could say anything – and what could she say? – he was gone, running up the steps. She heard the door slam.

He didn't come back. His men were giving her the evils, but they didn't dare say anything. She crept back to the flat at dawn, but he wasn't there. An empty glass and a tell-tale smudge of white powder on the table were the only evidence he'd been there. His black speedster was gone. She waited a couple of hours, then, fear fluttering in her belly, she made her way back to the club. It was quiet. Silent cleaners. The piano player idly practising. A couple of Tony's goons hanging about.

'No Tony?' one asked.

She was just shaking her head when the door slammed.

There, standing at the top of the stairs, was Tony.

She sagged into a chair. He was alright.

But then he turned to her, and she saw horror in his face. It wasn't alright. *He knew*. She half rose in her chair, but his gaze forced her back down.

'What's up, Tony?' cried someone. 'You look like you've seen a ghost!'

Tony glanced up, waved his hand as if to swat a fly, then looked back at her.

'Yeah. I think I have.' He sat down heavily. 'Get me a drink. A real drink – straight up.'

A whiskey was brought, and he drank it down.

Still looking right at her, Tony began to speak, 'I went straight back to the flat, scored a line and I was flying. Took my speedster out for a spin. I was off the dial, on a toot! I was on the crest of a wave, and then, from out nowhere this Rolls Royce Silver Ghost swung onto the road in front of me. I was sore to be beaten by that old thing! I put my foot right down. I didn't care where I was going; all I cared about was beating that hayburner right outta Dodge. But no matter how fast my Black Hawk went, that Silver Ghost was always ahead. We drove on till dawn. Then she turned off the road, and I followed. There was a cottage up there, a real roses round the door, rocking chairs on the porch kinda place.

I pulled up, but when I looked around, the Silver Ghost was gone. It was real lonely. But then, from outta nowhere came this white dove, and I swear it was it was singing 'Painting the Clouds with Sunshine' – maybe it was the cocaine, I dunno, but that's what I heard. I followed it. We were in this garden full of sassafras trees, and as the sun came up the dove lit down by a tree and I saw a grave, fresh dug.

That bird, he told me a story – and I swear it's not the cocaine talking. It sang of men coming in the dark of night.' Tony paused, rubbed his head. 'Short story, guys: it was a rub out. They'd knocked off the man and his kid. Left the moll alone.'

He looked straight at Nell. She tried to rise, but he was there, his hands gripping her wrists, and she was just a girl in the end. No matter how she struggled, she couldn't break free.

'And that dove, he said that the moll cut off her hair and changed her name – from Nellie to Bill. Ain't that right – Billy boy?'

'You're mad!' she whispered.

But it was too late. He pulled at her jacket, and her shirt buttons popped with the force of it.

'See here, boys. Billy's no Bill – he's a broad.'

They all stared at her bound breasts, and, gathering the fabric back, she collapsed to the floor, sobbing.

'Who did it, Nell?' Tony's voice was gentle now, and he knelt beside her, hand lightly on her shoulder. Its comfort brought the words spilling out.

'It was my stepmother! She hated Jake – he was a Fiore, of course she hated him. Told us that no Camerano was marrying a Fiore, wanted me to marry her nephew – but Jake and me married anyway. My Pa, he built us that cottage way out in the sticks to hide us, and we were happy, me and Jake and little Sammy. That night ... she didn't dare touch me, 'cos of what my Pa might do. I couldn't go to him – it'd break his heart, cause a feud. So I came here for protection ...'

'And they really killed your kid?'

'They pulled him from me ... and, after, I felt him die in my arms ...'

Tony shook his head.

'That's not right. Boys, get out there and do it!'

It was in the next day's paper. Ma Camerano had been found in her apartment with a bullet or six through her brains. Nobody was claiming the murder, but the papers dismissed it as just another gangster killing, and the city sure had enough of them.

When Nell saw the news, she wept.

She wept too at the gowns that had appeared overnight in the flat. Beautiful things, all silk and beads. She fingered a peach silk number, then turned away and dressed herself back in her man's suit once more.

That night Tony appeared with a bottle of champagne and a ring box.

'Will you? Will you say it'll be wedding bells for you and me?'

'Why do you want to marry me, Tony? You don't want a woman at all.'

He shrugged. 'And you don't want a man. We'll do alright. I'll keep you safe, and you – you'll keep the girls off my back. We get along, don't we? I think you're a great, great girl. Come on, let's do it, let's spread a little happiness.'

There was something in her heart for him. But…

'No, Tony, I can't. It'd be a lie, and you know it. My baby died in my arms, and there's no getting over that. Tony, you're a sweet man, but there ain't no sweet man that's worth the salt of my tears, not after Jake. And – I've gotta get away. I don't want no more death.'

''Tain't no sin to marry without love, Nell. People do it all the time.'

She shook her head.

'No, Tony. Yours, mine, it's all just a short life of trouble. You're just looking at the world through rose-coloured glasses if you think this can work. So, please, just pay me what I'm owed, and let me go – and promise me this only: if my Pa should come asking, don't tell him what happened to me.'

After she'd gone, Tony stood by the window and watched as the slight figure with Eton-cropped yellow hair and a black suit walked away down the road until she was lost in the crowds. He leaned against the window and murmured, 'Am I blue? Ain't these tears in these eyes telling you?'

'The Famous Flower of Serving Men' (Child 106/Roud 199), as sung by Martin Carthy, is for me one of the most evocative and chilling traditional ballads. I've wanted to tell it myself since I first heard it aged about thirteen. The ballad was first recorded in Percy's Reliques *in 1765 but may well be much older. The cold violence of America's 1920s ganglands updates the barbarity of the tale and reminds us that these atrocities can happen at any time in any place.*

14

Shirt for a Shroud

A Retelling of the Ballad 'Scarborough Fair' by Nimue Brown

Are you going to Scarborough Fair?
Parsley, sage, rosemary, and thyme;
Remember me to the one who lives there,
For once she was a true love of mine.

ANON, Yorkshire

We're wandering around the psychic fair, both of us looking for the genuine article, but for different reasons. My advantage is that I can see who is talking to ghosts. My beautiful Edward's advantage is that he can more reliably get sense out of the psychics. It all takes a lot of concentration on my part and I can only keep that going in short bursts. Especially with all the guilt and pain washing about. His. Mine.

'How are you on missing persons?' he asks each unoccupied psychic we encounter.

They offer him tarot readings, crystal ball gazing, and one suggests a shamanic counselling session. He keeps looking. He's restless, the need for answers carved into his face, grief lines like ritual scarification. A dreadful initiation, this has been.

'Do you have a photo?' one of them finally says.

He has a whole album of shots. Me laughing. Me looking at things. Me with a crown of flowers. I had no idea how often he'd photographed me unawares, before we started going to events like this.

'When did she go missing?'

His voice catches in his throat as he speaks. 'Back in the winter.' He's said it all so many times – first to the police, then to people like this woman, with her calculating eyes set in a cream-cake face. 'We quarrelled, she took off. The car turned up, but not her. The police ...'

'They couldn't help?'

'No.'

'It happens.'

I give her time to weigh him up, to find him genuine. He's not a stalker spinning a lie; he's a man in real trouble. When she seems ready, I speak to her. 'Please tell him that I'm dead.'

She looks in my general direction, but not at me – apparently she can hear but not see. Her face is all too readable – this is the last thing she wants to announce to a potential client. However, as she can hear me, it's too good an opportunity to ignore, and I have to try. 'At least tell him you can help him. His name is Edward, he's thirty-four and he works in finance.' She relays this part, and it startles him enough to stay put.

There's a glimmer of hope in his eyes. 'Can you help me? Can you tell me where she is?'

The psychic glances to my right, but I get the impression she's trying to communicate with me, without speaking. There's a terrible irony here.

'Please tell him that I always meant to come back. I was just cross and needed to let off steam. I didn't mean to leave him like this. He shouldn't blame himself so much.'

She shakes her head. To say this would be to make it pretty clear that I'm dead, and it looks like she can't bring herself to do it. Instead, she keeps Edward busy with empty questions and hollow soothing noises as I shout at her, trying to get her attention. She's impervious to threats, curses, pleading and promises. I guess she's heard it all before, which isn't a comforting idea. Why won't she help me?

Next thing I know, she's booking Edward in for a proper consultation and I can't stay focused any longer.

Edward is a creature of habit, which makes haunting him fairly straightforward. So long as I can keep track of the time, all I have to do is tune in every now and then to make sure he's behaving normally. It infuriates me that he can neither hear nor see me. I can't help but feel he could, if only he made a bit more effort. Even on the really good days, when I'm able to move small objects, he's oblivious to my presence.

The consultation comes round and I go with him. Angel art and too many cushions. Maya Angelica works out of her own home, which could not be more clichéd as a space if she tried. It's easier for me to stay focused when I'm feeling something, and as she mostly talks bland drivel I struggle to hold onto my anger and my presence. I fade in and out. Somehow, the bland drivel turns into an imperative to do some kind of spiritual penance. Edward is lapping this stuff up, which makes me cross, which helps. He has to make a shirt for me? It must be hand sewn, and so neat you can barely see the seams. When he's done that, he's to come back for another consultation.

'Will this help get her back?' He's far too keen. It troubles me.

'This is what has to be done,' the whey-faced psychic pronounces.

When he rises to leave, she hisses, 'Stay', so that I hear and he does not. I stay. Edward leaves. Psychic-Maya sashays back.

'Still here?'

'Yes.'

'You're his missing, dead lover, right? Haunting him.'

'I'm trying to help him.'

'You're killing him,' she says.

How dare she? 'The uncertainty is killing him,' I reply. 'He needs closure, why won't you help us?'

'He needs to let go and move on, but you aren't letting him do that.'

'Fuck you.'

'He needs to grieve,' she insists.

I go, and I watch and wait as the love of my life spends his spare time learning how to sew. It takes him months to do the ridiculous task, and the resulting shirt is not a thing of symmetry or beauty. Back he goes for another phony consultation, and the psychic-bitch tells him he's got to wash the shirt in a holy well, and dry it by hanging it from the branches of a blackthorn.

'I can tell you how to find my body,' I say to her.

She doesn't react. Surely she must want this? She'd be famous and Edward could bury me, and sort out the nightmarish paperwork problems the missing cause, and he would know that I am here and that I am never really going to leave him. I only want to take care of him. Why won't she listen to me?

I tell her anyway. 'I went up into the mountains on my own. I know it wasn't entirely clever, but I've walked in far worse conditions than that, before. I was unlucky, that's all. I really thought by now some other walker would have found my remains.'

She ignores me.

Edward takes the ridiculous shirt home, purchases and studies an Ordnance Survey map and has his surreal laundry job done by the end of the week.

'You're going to need access to some land, for the next bit,' she tells him.

Edward laughs at this. When did he last laugh? There's colour in his face again and I remember how much I loved him, wanted him, and how often he drove me round the bend. Ours was never an easy relationship.

'I Googled this stuff. I thought it sounded familiar, although you've gone easy on me. Seams in the shirt, water in the well. You aren't going to specify the land has to be between the water and the shore, are you?'

'You don't need it to be impossible. You just needed it to keep you busy.'

'What is this about?' He's curious, not angry. I want him to be angry over how she's cheated him.

'It's an old cure for obsession. You know … we don't always get to find out what really happened when someone dies. Even when there are answers, well, those often lead to more questions anyway. Finding your lost girlfriend wouldn't have healed you, but you did need to let her go. It's hard to do that when all you can focus on is your own doubt and fear. Sewing is much more useful.'

'So there wasn't any magic in the whole shirt thing?'

He seems forlorn now. I want to comfort him. I want to comfort me, to feel the warmth of him and smell his skin.

'The song is old magic,' she says. 'Two ways of going about it. When the dead come back, you set them impossible tasks to complete so that they can't take you until they've finished. Of course they never finish. Or you set the living near-impossible tasks to stop them pining away and following the dead.'

'You think she's dead, then?'

The psychic monstrosity nods. 'Was she a mountain climber?'

His jaw drops. Not that it would have been hard for a charlatan to find this out, during these last few months. He's so hopelessly gullible.

'She took off in a rage after you quarrelled and came to grief somewhere in walking distance of where the car was found.'

I scream at her. 'Why couldn't you just tell him this when I asked you to? Why keep him hanging on all this time? Focused on you. Is it just about the money? Oh, you're a piece of work, aren't you?'

She ignores me and speaks to Edward. 'You needed to be ready to stop hoping.'

'Yes, you're right. It's tough, but you're right.'

I feel betrayed.

'If I'd told you all this before, you could never have let her go. You'd have wanted me to help you talk to her.'

He smiles. Heartrending and sweet. Smiles agreement. Bastard. This is not what I wanted. This was not supposed to happen.

'Hungry ghosts,' says Maya Angelica. 'They can't move on. The dead ones who follow the living, who show up at psychic fairs trying to get heard ... they want to eat your life. I can't speak that truth to a person who is still raw. But I think you can hear it now. In life, these people are takers. Users. They steal your joy and energy. Psychic vampires if you will. In death, they only get worse.'

I want Edward to argue with her. Why is he not defending me? I was the best thing that ever happened to him. I am his soul mate. He owes me more loyalty than this.

'I felt so guilty. I couldn't think about anything properly,' he says at last. 'My fault for driving her away. My fault something went wrong. But each day it got that little bit easier to breathe, and I felt guilty about that, too. I would never have wished her dead, but at the same time, I'm so glad she's out of my life, and it's taken me until now to admit it. Does that make me an awful person?'

'It makes you a wiser man who has some hope for a future.'

He smiles again, and his whole face is softer and more relaxed than it's looked in years. I hate seeing him happy without me. I don't want him moving on. I want to wrap my arms around his neck and oblige him to carry me for the rest of his life. That's what true love means, isn't it? Never letting go.

'There's still hope for you,' the psychic says. Edward has gone, I realise. I've not been following things properly. She must be talking to me.

'You can change, even in death. You can choose to do better. Let him go. Let your jealousy go and move on. Simple as that.'

But I don't want to let go. I walked out on him that winter morning because I wanted to scare him into realising that he can't live without me. None of this was supposed to happen. I don't want him to get over it. I want him to die of a broken heart. I want him to spend his whole life in abject misery, mourning for me and drowning in his guilt. I want to always be the most important thing for him.

But now he's gone out into the bright sunshine. I drift after him, towards the tourist-laden beach and the soft rhythm of waves. If he really loved me, he'd drown himself to be with me forever. Instead, he buys an ice cream.

If I had the means to touch him, I would flay the skin from his bones for this. I love him too much. I cannot let him go.

Are you going to Scarborough Fair? Remember me to one who lives there, for he once was a true love of mine.

As a lifelong folky, I can't remember a time when I didn't at least know the repeating lines in 'Scarborough Fair' (Roud S160449). As a child, the impossible tasks fascinated me. I was in my twenties when singer-songwriter Jon Harvison explained to me the relationship between this song, and the unquiet graves songs, and the idea that the impossible tasks are how you stop the dead from absconding with the living. In other related songs, the dead rise up more literally and the implications for the surviving lover aren't good, but this is the consequence of too-violent grief:

> *My lips are cold as clay, sweetheart,*
> *My breath smells heavy and strong,*
> *And if you kiss my lily-white lips,*
> *Your time would not be long.*
> *(Child 78)*

It's been on my mind to do something with these stories for a while, and this anthology offered the perfect motivation.

❧ 15 ❧

The Grand Gateway

A Retelling of the Ballad 'Barbara Allen' by Mark Hassall

O mother, mother, make my bed,
For his death hath quite undone me.
A hard-hearted creature that I was,
To slight one that lovd me so dearly;
I wish I had been more kinder to him,
The time of his life when he was near me.

ANON, Scotland

Allen Barber was as devoted as a priest to the Victorian Cemetery hidden within the city's leafy suburbia. Although he was a single man in his thirties he had never comfortably fitted into the clothes of an English city lifestyle, but loved Victorian frockcoats and period pocket watches. As a volunteer tour guide he dressed meticulously for the role in period mourning dress and finished off his costume with a polished black walking cane topped in silver. He was a popular choice as a guide and willingly offered up all he knew about the historic cemetery to the tourists who came looking for 'somewhere different' to visit during their city-break.

I didn't know him then. And I don't know if I ever really knew him. Like the dusty iron gates of an old tomb, his ways were closed. But his story stayed with me like one of the old tales, the ones that shift and twist depending on who tells them, but its core always stays the same.

One clear morning in late autumn Allen led his regular eleven o'clock group in the direction of the grand gateway at the heart of the cemetery. Holding his cane high, he threaded a path between some granite chest tombs covered with ivy and heavily laden with drops of dew. The month of November was a popular time for all the volunteers. The tour groups flocked to their cemetery, keen to hear a ghost story or two or, like yesterday evening's party, to walk the cemetery's old paths in a parade of glowing St Martin's Eve lanterns. He recalled the comforting light issuing from the many-coloured crepe globes, which had left a ruddy warm feeling within him rather than usual anxious urgency to complete the tour before closing time, when the blackened iron gates clanked together and were locked for the night to leave the dead in peace.

Suddenly, Allen's reverie was disturbed as he realised that the group had arrived at the impressive threshold to the central catacombs. The whole party looked on silently, waiting for him to continue the tour. Slightly embarrassed by this unusual loss of focus, Allen continued. 'So here we are at the grand gateway to the central catacombs! For the Victorian funeral party, movement through this passageway into the circular structure of sandstone tombs beyond would have been rather like a transition from one world to the next ...' said Allen, trying to recover himself. He looked over the group with a tight smile ...

Then a woman's voice called out from the back of the group: 'The gateway is very impressive. But why are there no yew trees nearby?' She fixed her gaze upon Allen with raised eyebrows, keen for an answer.

He recognised her to be a member of last evening's St Martin's festival, a young woman who had hung back at the end to press him with a stream of urgent questions about the cemetery. Yesterday her heavy black duffle coat and woollen hat obscured her figure, but now, with her jacket open, Allen noticed she was dressed as if for summer in a white blouse finely embroidered with sunflowers and skinny pale blue jeans. Her white-blonde hair framed a heart-shaped face and fell across her shoulders like a waterfall.

Allen pulled his waistcoat straight, his hands pressing down on the creases as if ironing out his irritation. He took a sharp breath. 'Good question madam! But we need to move the tour onwards as I have another group at half-past twelve. I can answer further questions at the end of our tour. Please will you all follow me?' said Allen as he lifted up his cane and made a little flurry in the air with its silver top, and beckoned the tour forward. As he turned towards the twin stone pillars of the gateway, Allen noticed the look of disappointment in the young woman's face as she joined the line of tourists walking into the catacombs.

A few days later as Allen counted out and logged the entrance takings for the day, another guide passed him a small folded piece of paper. Opening out the paper he noticed the familiar format of the cemetery's volunteer application form. It was a simple process to apply and he recalled that the format hadn't changed since he had applied himself so long ago. This form had been completed by a Miss Willow West. Her application read: *I want to socialise and improve my knowledge of the local area after moving to the city from the West of England.* Allen marked the application in the volunteer logbook and sealed the form in an envelope along with the day's takings as the bell from the cemetery gatehouse announced closing time.

One week later Allen broke away from the tour guides' shared tea and melted into the undergrowth to thread a path between crying angels trailed with ivy and lichen-crusted tombs, to return back to the terrace catacombs. In summer he loved to take his tea and read there, bathed in the soft golden light from the line of reassessed oculi in the ceiling above.

Today, as he entered the passageway the air smelled moist and earthy and the light from above was pale and pregnant with water vapour. Nonetheless, Allen reached behind the entrance door, pulled out a striped deckchair and settled down to his tea. He popped open the flask's seal which echoed down the corridor, the steam rising to mingle with the wet mist. In the silence of the stone corridor the sound of feet scratching over the gravel floor startled him.

Then, in a soft voice, a young woman called out from the doorway behind Allen. 'I hope you don't mind my intruding ...' said the voice with a suppressed giggle. 'You were sitting so still I might have mistaken you for a ghost.' The voice whispered quietly, as if hushed in reverence.

Allen looked up at the slim silhouette of a woman's frame in the doorway. His eyes looked past her as if he was peering into the distance and then he came to with an apologetic jolt and shifted nervously in his seat. 'Please excuse me. I'm not used to visitors here,' said Allen and beckoned her in with a nervous smile.

The woman withdrew her hand from her jeans pocket and reached out to Allen, who uncharacteristically shook her hand. She looked up in surprise from Allen's own cold hand. 'I'm Willow by the way. It's my first month volunteering here. I've noticed you skulking off at teatime and I wondered where you went. Do you remember me? You didn't answer my question about the yew trees. Would you have some time now?' she asked in a friendly tone.

Allen paused. He was flattered by Willow's request but felt uneasy about being sought out in his private domain. He pulled out another chair, brushed it down and invited Willow to sit as he began to answer her question in full.

Willow listened intently to Allen, who experienced her silent attention not as an irritation but an invitation. Under her soft gaze he found himself sharing how he visited the catacombs to 'commune with the dead', a long-dead Victorian practice but one which he had discovered as a way to remind himself of his own mortality.

The light had begun to draw dim around the doorway but it was only when the faint chimes from the cemetery gatehouse reached Allen and Willow in the terrace catacombs that they knew how long they had been speaking together.

From then on Allen and Willow passed many a late autumn afternoon together in the same manner. While all around them was sinking into decay, a flowering of love unfurled itself between them, and the pale stone charnel house became, in the closeness their company, a palace of retreat.

Allen left the cosseted warmth of the railway station and pushed his hands deeper into the welcome pockets of his frockcoat. There was harshness in the cold February air and an early frost clung to the grass, a last remnant of winter.

On his arrival at the cemetery gatehouse Allen found the usual group of volunteers standing in a tight huddle around the small fire grate. One member of the group silently looked over to Allen, his gaze hesitant, not quite meeting his eyes, and pointed to the mahogany letter-holder fixed to the wall opposite. Allen noticed a pale pink vellum envelope slotted into his message holder. In neat black ink the envelope was simply addressed, *To Allen, a friend to our Willow*. Allen slowly lifted it out; his fingers tentatively traced along the edges of the envelope before quickly breaking the seal to discover a hand-written letter:

Dear Allen,

I hope you are the man my daughter speaks about. Willow has been fighting with cancer these past years and has recently experienced a sudden relapse in her symptoms. She has been urgently admitted to hospital. Over the past weeks, when she has the strength, Willow has spoken fondly about the cemetery and her work. She has requested that we inform the group of volunteers but has particularly asked for you to visit. Please don't disappoint her. The details are enclosed.

Yours faithfully,
Tom West.

For a moment Allen stood motionless. Then, with a measure of calmness a surgeon would have been proud of, he let out a long breath and neatly folded up the letter.

One by one he heard the footfalls of the volunteers as they quietly left him staring into the fire-grate, turning over his emotions like glowing embers with the singular question: how could she have held this from him? It was only the resonance of the gatehouse bell that pushed past all his fury and recalled Allen to himself. Looking up at the wall-clock he realised the time and, placing the now folded envelope within the breast pocket of his frockcoat, he left the room to prepare for his eleven o'clock tour.

The rest the day passed like any other. Allen clung onto his routine like a life raft but he soon began to imagine the questions Willow might have asked had she been there.

At lunch, Allen took his usual walk outside the cemetery walls when his attention was caught by a flash of sunlight through the trees followed quickly by an image of Willow in her purple tights and green suede boots, excitedly kicking up the tinder dry leaves from the path. The envelope still blazed in the pocket of his coat. At the end of the day with his anger now cold in the fire-grate, Allen got up from his familiar seat in the damp catacombs, having decided to visit Willow in hospital.

The popular city hospital was one of the country's main cancer services. It was a quiet Sunday morning and Allen passed through the hospital entrance. His hand clutched tightly onto a map of the hospital site, as he looked frantically back and forth between the map and each of the numerous empty corridors. Eventually Allen settled on a route towards the 'Yellow Zone', which gave way to warmly lit corridors with soft pastel furnishings, but nothing could dissolve away the clinical smell that assaulted his senses.

Finally, Allen arrived at the entrance to the ward and was led to Willow's bed, framed by a light-blue curtain. On the other side he could hear the sound of soft breathing. Allen passed his hand lightly along the fabric, his fingers fumbling, trying to find a way in. Finally, he found an edge and peeled back the curtain to find Willow much changed since he had last seen her.

Her thin frame was easily hidden under a tangle of starched bed sheets, her blonde hair a turbulent pool surrounding her face. Willow stirred in her bed then opening her half-lidded eyes she turned to

Allen and offered him the warmest smile he had even been given. It reached across to him like a pale sun might cover over a field of frost in early winter.

'Thanks for coming. Take a pew. It's the best seat in the house', said Willow, playfully drawing attention to a very sensible chair next to her bed.

Allen nodded and sat on the edge of the chair. 'Your ward was quite difficult to find. The whole place is like a rabbit warren! It was so quiet I started to wonder where all the patients were,' said Allen.

'I'm glad you came,' said Willow.

'I asked my Dad to write to you as I was feeling really tired that week. I wondered what it might have been like to get a letter from him, my Dad. Was it too weird?' said Willow with a mock painful expression.

Allen did not answer, but instead looked around the ward surrounded by so much clinical equipment, as an orchestra of shrill beeps and low pulses filled the silence between them.

Willow frowned and then broke the silence. 'How did the volunteers take my news?' she asked, trying to catch a glance from Allen.

Allen finally looked at Willow, 'I haven't really spoken to them much … I went away for one week and found you had left when I came back,' he said, curtly. 'I would imagine it was quite a surprise for everyone,' he said.

Willow let her head fall back into her pillow. 'OK … I guess you should have an explanation,' she said with a sigh. 'Allen I know you're angry, but you don't start talking about your illness when you are first getting to know someone. At first I thought you would be a great source of information, but as we spoke together I grew to love our time together and … I learned to love you Allen. You have such a lovely and lonely soul. I'm about to start my next phase of chemo. It would be lovely to see more of you. Do you think you might come back?' Willow asked. Her voice sounded casual but the plea was clearly in her eyes.

A distant look settled on Allen's face. 'Willow … I'm not much good at this sort of thing,' said Allen apologetically.

'But Allen I'm not asking …'

He shifted uncomfortably in his seat. 'I know. Maybe ... I need to think about it ... Look, I don't want to be rude but I should be going. I have an early tour this afternoon.' His fingers fumbled absent-mindedly with his pocket watch.

Willow regarded him and something in her face seemed to shrink. 'Okay. No worries.' She tried to smile. 'See you around then.'

Allen nodded and slowly turned to leave. 'Yes, see you around,' he said over his shoulder and silently slipped through the curtain.

Allen walked away from the hospital that evening feeling numb and unreal. However, it wasn't long before he returned to the cemetery to continue with his tours and slipped back into the comfort of his old routine.

One day, as Allen was leading a tour towards one his favourite parts of the cemetery, silence came over the group behind him. Allen turned on his heels, his long coat in a flurry, as the bell from the gatehouse began to toll. The great iron gates opened inwards to allow a line of polished black cars to drive slowly through, their weighted tyres cracking upon the gravel beneath. The tour group bowed their heads respectively. Each mournful knell of the bell was an assault on the trusted walls Allen had built around himself. If a member of the tour group had looked at his face they would have noticed Allen's gaze was fixed upon the funeral hearse, where the name 'Willow' was spelled out alongside the coffin in flowers. The large iron gates swung back and closed as he finally beckoned the tour party forward in a lacklustre manner.

Allen's gait was unsteady, like a man who had lost his footing in the world, as he made his way slowly between some fallen headstones and under a curtain of ivy.

'So what happened to Allen ... ?' asked one of the tourists.

The tour guide cleared his throat and continued. 'After Willow's funeral, Allen spent less time in the eastern catacombs, choosing instead to take his tea here by her graveside. I stumbled upon him once as he nursed his flask of tea and we got talking. We spoke every now and then and one day he told me his story. Maybe this was why he chose to appoint me as the executor of his will. As he instructed, I purchased a plot beside Willow's grave and ... here he lies.' The tour guide pointed towards two graves lain against the walls of the cemetery, one was furnished with a red rose bush in full flower, whilst the other lay in a tangle of green bramble.

This story is based on the ballad of 'Barbara Allen' (Child 84/Roud 54) in which a young woman rejects an opportunity for love but deeply regrets it later. I was drawn to this ballad because I recognised within it complex themes of love and grief. I was also interested to learn that the ballad is well travelled and versions of it have been found across the British Isles, North America and even a source from my own local area in Dartmoor.

❦ 16 ❦

Mermaid in Aspic

A Retelling of the Ballads 'The Twa Sisters', 'Binnorie' and 'The Bonny Swans' by Chrissy Derbyshire

> *There were two sisters, they went playing,*
> *With a hie downe downe a downe-a*
> *To see their father's ships come sayling in.*
> *With a hy downe downe a downe-a*
> *And when they came unto the sea-brym,*
> *The elder did push the younger in.*

ANON

I blame Ophelia. She was my first, my most-beloved idol of romantic drowning. When, too young, I read how her clothes bore her up in the stream like a siren before drinking the dark water and pulling her down, something in my heart clicked into place. After that, one or two nights in a month, I would dream I was drowned. Not a nightmare. A release. It came in many forms. Sometimes I would sink into the deepest dark, with an eternity of blue water over my head. Sometimes I would lie facedown in the shallows, tasting salt and sand, letting the tide fill my hair with pearls and diamonds as I breathed in saltwater. Most often there was a river. When it actually happened (not my own drowning, but another's), my first feeling was neither repulsion nor terror but love.

Catherine played guitar down in the underpass. Every note played out twice, once from the body of the instrument, once from the damp tiled walls. She played 'O-o-ver-ver the-the Rain-ain-bow-ow' to people who kept their faces down and shuffled quickly for fear of muggers. In her head she was accompanied by flutes and a cello and she hoped her playing conveyed this. It didn't.

Catherine played for a handful of coins, but her sights were set on something less tangible. She was waiting for a moment. A second of eye contact with a stranger that said, 'Thank you. This was what I needed. You have spoken to me. You have told me the truth.' She had no doubt that this would happen. Life had afforded her the opportunity to learn to play. Why, if not to connect? Why anything, if not to use it to change a life or a mind? Catherine lived and felt in Technicolor. She thought in black and white.

When she felt the shadows stretching out their hands over the frets, covering her eyes, turning the tunnel chill and unwelcoming, she packed up her guitar and left. Unafraid of the dark, on intimate terms with it, she headed for the river. It was a longer route home, but it was the route she always took. This river was her companion. She knew its moods: saw its best days, swollen with rain and rushing; saw its worst, reduced to a sticky trickle of mud. She felt the joy of shivering silvery fish, laughed at the tickling feet and beaks of herons, hissed at the pain of rust and plastic. Tonight it was slow and fine, deep aquamarine shot with white under a perfect half-moon. In the distance, Catherine could see a swan, floating, blue in the darkness. She stopped to look.

The swan curled strangely. Was it sleeping with a head under its wing? Sleep-swimming? Was it fishing? The darkness gave it the illusion of extraordinary length: a swan reflected in a fairground mirror, still beautiful but weirdly elongated. Now that it was approaching, she wondered *was* it a swan? It seemed to be trailing pondweed like mermaid hair behind it. The strands shone in the moonlight, beautiful. The swan looked like Ophelia. The swan … looked like … A girl trapped in a paperweight. A mermaid in aspic. A wide-eyed princess in a glass coffin.

Catherine knelt down and gently caught the drowned girl. There was barely any weight to her. 'Hello,' whispered Catherine, over the girl's parted lips. She pressed her blazing cheek against the girl's cold one. She dragged the body from the river. After many long moments of staring into the glassy eyes and feeling river water seep into her lap, she blinked twice and felt for the girl's wallet. She recovered a watercolour driving license, half drained away, as though already at the business of marking her death.

Who are you? This waterlogged card calls you Mary Pitt, born in 1980 in the dead of winter. I see your mother, screaming in the throes of birth, willing you into the world, not knowing you would be gone from it so soon. Her last. I feel you were her last. The baby of the family. The innocent. Coddled, perhaps, but unspoiled. I see your siblings, one, two, three: two brothers, one sister. Your sister. I will call her Ann. She feels like an Ann. Your sister loved you until you angered her. Then she drowned you. You would not kill yourself. You are too beautiful, too sane. No, it was Ann. I see her so clearly that I cannot have invented her. I see it all in your eyes.

Let me tell you your story.

Ann was not a beauty. Some called her striking, with her sharp hooked nose and sharper eyes, but no one would call her lovely. Nevertheless, she was quick-witted and smart and fiery, and she had her share of interest from men. But she was not interested in men. She was interested in *one* man. She liked him against her better judgement. He was not especially brilliant, not especially witty. He was only good-looking and kind, and at first it was enough for her to laugh at herself for letting her gaze linger.

Then he fell for Mary, and Ann could no longer laugh. Mary. Younger, softer, golden-haired and gamine. Men fell at her feet. She could pick them like chocolates from the box. Nor did she gloat. It would have been better if she rubbed it in Ann's face. Then, at least, she could hate her. But Mary seemed not to notice that she was effortlessly loved. Ann found herself watching them compulsively, the way one does something horrible yet compelling. When they kissed, she glared. When they whispered, she muttered. But she kept her anger from you, Mary, didn't she? She tried to hide it.

Then, one night, this night, the sisters were walking along the river and Mary was talking effusively about her new love. He was so attentive. So devoted. So very handsome. And Ann – I can understand her! – she felt the bitterness rising, choking her. And she glanced down and saw how close to the river Mary was walking. She felt herself swaying towards her sister. Just imagining. Just imagining how it would be if she were no longer in the world. And perhaps it was a moment of madness or perhaps it was an accident brought on by skirting the edge of danger, but you were in the water, Mary, in the water with weeds tangling round your ankles, natural as a swan in the cold clear stream. Mary cried to her sister to help her. Ann stared. Then she spoke and was stung by the coldness of her own words. 'Give him up,' she said. 'Give him to me and I'll help you.'

Mary was crying and shivering, bewildered. 'Bill?' she said. 'I can't ... he's not mine to give! I can't just give a person to you, even if I wanted to! What are you saying? Get me out! I'm freezing and I'm caught!' In her passion she lost her footing and her head went briefly under the water. She came up coughing. 'Help!' she called. You called. But Ann had gone.

In that short time she was no longer visible. You were alone and it was starting to get dark. Maybe you called for help some more. Certainly you struggled, scrabbled for the riverbank. It was ridiculous, you thought, to drown in a little river like this. But it has hidden undertows, tangling plants, a bed of quicksand, and your foot was stuck and the river was pulling at you, and you kept going under again and again until you were more water than air.

That was how I found you. I cannot see what happened to Ann. My vision stops there. But I know you, beautiful Mary. I know your story. I know it and I will tell it. *We* will tell it. Where are those scissors?

Alone in the dark but for the dead body of Mary Pitt, Catherine lovingly snipped away a lock of the girl's dull-gold hair. Humming softly to herself, she opened her guitar case and took out the old, beat-up acoustic guitar. With deft fingers she wrapped the hair around the strings, binding one to the other. Then she stroked the girl's head, kissed her brow, and left for home.

The morning dawned blinding and already hot. Catherine carried her guitar, now threaded with gold, to the underpass. She had a new song to sing – one of a sister scorned, of jealousy and madness, of an angel drowned in a river, a woman turned to a swan turned to a guitar. She barely registered the footsteps as they approached her. It was only when they slowed that she clocked them. Usually people hurried through here, scared of the dark. The feet stopped in front of her. A woman's feet. She stopped singing – the song had just finished, anyway – and looked up into a face. She smiled, overwhelmed. There was that look, that look of recognition. 'Thank you,' it said. 'This was what I needed. You have spoken to me. You have told me the truth.'

'Thank you,' said Catherine, still smiling, as the woman reached into her jacket to produce a police badge.

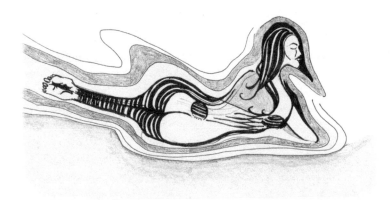

'Catherine Ann Pitt?' asked the woman.

Oh.

Oh, yes.

That was it.

Catherine played guitar down in the underpass.

Ann played with drowned dolls.

It is so difficult to hold your head together sometimes, with the water always closing above it. Under the water you are preoccupied. Under the water, the people up above are obscured. They might be anyone, doing anything. They might be dancing, or falling apart.

'I blame Ophelia,' Catherine said.

I approached this story with little idea how I might adapt it, except that I wanted it to feel magical without having any magic in it. Reading several versions of the original ballad ('The Two Sisters', Child 10/Roud 8), which I knew initially from Loreena McKennitt's soft folk interpretation, two things struck me. The first was that to remove the magic from the story would make it a very different beast indeed. The second was that the most intriguing character in the story – the 'false sister Ann' – was treated in a typically one-dimensional way. Like many, if not most, ballad characters, she was little more than a cipher for a particular quality – falseness.

I am interested in the idea of delusion and false perception, and my work frequently touches on these. I find that it is possible to evoke the same uncanny feeling that magic affords by portraying a world as seen through the warped lens of madness. However, I wanted to present the character of Catherine Ann (two names, two personalities) without judgement or pity. I hope that I have made her, like any person with their inner life exposed, strange, sometimes frightening, but ultimately relatable and even somewhat sympathetic. She is broken, fractured, potentially cruel, but she feels deeply and wishes only to create and taste beauty. Like the mermaid of the title, she is by her very nature wrapped up with music, love, and violence, though she only achieves one successfully. So this is her story, retaining the river, the swan, the drowning for love, the confusion between female body and musical instrument, and the song that tells the truth. Take it as you will.

✂ 17 ✂

The Wind Shall Blow

A Retelling of the Ballads 'The Three Ravens' and 'The Twa Corbies' by David Metcalfe

Downe in yonder greene field,
There lies a knight slain under his shield.
His hounds they lie downe at his feete,
So well they can their master keepe.

ANON, England

The black feathers brushed across his blood-crusted face. He tried to raise his right hand – no good. His right arm felt so very heavy. His left arm, pinned beneath him, was stiff and throbbing – broken? The bird flapped down and landed beside him, raising a small puff of dust. *Corvus corax* – common raven. The raven cocked its head, opened its beak. 'Kraaak.' It hopped closer to his face, 'Aark, kraaak.'

Craig woke.

'Krak, krak.' Small arms fire, some way away.

Craig sat up, lifted the mosquito net over his head and rubbed his eyes with the tips of his fingers. That same bloody dream again. Wiping the sweat from his forehead with the back of his right hand, Craig stood up and slowly stretched his stiff arms. Picking up his binoculars he stepped outside the tent. The breeze cooled his face and bare shoulders.

Craig had grown used to the heat and the dust. The week in Camp Bastion, to acclimatise and to be briefed on the situation in Afghanistan, and on progress with Operation Herrick, seemed a hazy memory now. His awareness had long-since been hijacked by the harsh day-to-day reality of life in Patrol Base Blenheim, with its steady, basic, mainly monotonous but sometimes manic rhythm. Each day strangely the same but different: Groundhog Day with a twist. Sleep, shit, eat, get shot at, patrol, search, get shot at, eat, sleep ... still, three months in now – three more to go. Then back home for some leave, and Angie.

Raven-haired, blue-eyed Angie – what might she be doing now? Probably planning a night out with her mates somewhere on the Bigg Market, or maybe she'd just be having a quiet night in with her mam in Jesmond. Craig suppressed the rising half-thought that she might be seeing someone else. Angie's last letter had been difficult for him to read and to respond to, after their phone conversation when he was at Camp Bastion. Craig recalled what they'd said on the phone.

'Hi Angie, love.'

'Craig? I cannot hear you very well. Are you OK?'

'Sure, fine. Not sleeping too good but getting used to the weather. It almost got to thirty degrees yesterday. A bit chilly at night though. How are you?'

'Oh, fine, fine. Mam's got me some new curtains for the flat. And it's OK at work now I'm more settled. It's taken a while. They're a good crowd at work, mind – up for a laugh. How's the bird watching? Seen anything new?'

'Not really had time for that – too much else going on. I should have more chance when I'm off into the action. Only a couple more days here now, then I won't be able to phone you – only write.'

'OK. OK ... Craig?'

'Yes.'

'There's something I want to talk about – about you and me – something I've wanted to say for a while. Maybe it's not a good idea over the phone just now. It's hard. But there's never time to talk properly, face-to-face – with you down in Essex with the regiment and me up here in Newcastle. And when you do come up, it's only ever for a short while, and there's never been the right time to sit down and have a proper talk. Craig? Are you there?'

'Yes.'

'Well, I think maybe we should give ourselves a bit of space for a while. You know, not rush things or commit to anything.'

'What do you mean?'

'Well, it's hard for me, you doing what you're doing.'

'What do you mean?'

'It's the army, Craig. It's the bomb disposal work, all the waiting and the worrying. It's you being away out of the country for six months at a time, then you being away down south most of the time when you're back. It's hard, Craig – hard for me. And it must be hard for you, me being up here.'

'I thought you said you were OK with all that. We talked it over, ages ago. When we first got together, we talked about it.'

'Yes, but living with it for real is different. It's not been easy.'

'It's not just that, is it?'

'What do you mean?'

'Have you met someone else? Met someone at work?'

'No. Not really.'

'What do you mean?'

'No. Well, not exactly. Listen, Craig, I just want a bit of time to think about things, about what I'm doing, about where I'm going. Listen, please. It's not that I don't care about you. It's just that I'm not sure.'

'I'm not sure I know what you mean.'

'I'm not sure I know what I mean either, Craig. Listen, I'll write, OK?'

'OK.'

Angie's letter had arrived ten days later:

Dear Craig

I hope you are well and in good spirits?

I'm writing to say that I've been thinking a lot about the two of us and how we're getting on at the moment. We've had a lot of good times and a lot of fun over the last few years.

But us being apart a lot of the time is making it hard to keep our relationship going. At least I'm finding it hard. I don't really know how you're finding it as you don't speak much about it when we are together.

Anyway, I think it would be best for both of us if we stopped seeing each other for a while.

I do care for you, Craig, but I'm not sure I'm in love with you anymore.

Angie

Craig had written back a month later:

Dearest Angie

I don't really know what to say after getting your last letter – except that I love you.

I know it's hard for you when I'm away, but try to think about the fun and the good times. If you can find it in your heart to stand by me for a couple more years, then I can leave the army with a good trade and we can be together properly.
All my love,

Craig

Craig gripped his binoculars tightly in his right hand and walked briskly across the compound to the sangar wall. The strengthening breeze whipped up the dust into little whirlwinds. Climbing up to the parapet he positioned himself carefully, mindful of possible snipers, raised the binoculars to his eyes and gazed out across the arid scrubland. Focusing on a clump of bushes about a quarter of a mile away, he watched and waited.

Craig's mood calmed. He knew there were about 130 different species of bird in Afghanistan. He wanted to see some of the rare and endangered ones while his tour of duty lasted. So far, over the past three months, he'd seen two very rare falcons – a male *falco cherrug*, commonly called a saker falcon, and a female *falco vespertinus*, or red-footed falcon. Only last week Craig thought he might have seen a *neophron pernopterus*, an Egyptian vulture, and on the endangered list. But the bird had been too far away and the evening light too dim for him to be sure.

Craig steadily scanned the scrub and brushwood for signs of bird life. After a quarter of an hour, seeing nothing of particular interest, he lowered the binoculars and looked up. Not too far above him a pair of common ravens tracked across the sky from left to right. Craig looked away. Bad luck, he thought. He checked his wristwatch – time to get ready for the late afternoon patrol.

Now fully kitted-up, Craig joined his section of Explosive Ordinance Disposal specialists assembling by the two Land Rovers. As commander of the section and search team leader, Corporal Craig Armstrong briefed the other seven men about the target village they were going to search and about the intelligence they'd received about possible Taliban infiltration. Then he double-checked he'd got his morphine shot and adjusted his metal-jacket before climbing into the back of one of the vehicles, carefully placing his SA80 rifle and his detector next to him. Mick sat down beside him while Jock, the team's sniffer dog lay down, unconcerned and calmly panting, on the metal floor at their feet. Craig leaned down and tousled the dog's head as the others piled in around them. The Land Rovers set off.

They drove for about three quarters of an hour south-west along the main roadway before turning north onto a rough track for a couple of miles towards their destination – a small village of five single-storey houses surrounded by neglected fields bounded by low stone walls. A few shrubs and trees provided sparse shade for several goats.

The two Land Rovers pulled up at the edge of the settlement and the men climbed swiftly and watchfully out of the vehicles. A woman and two young boys appeared in the doorway of one of the houses. Mick approached the woman slowly, with Jock padding along at his side. He said a few words to her in Dari about the men wanting to look around the village. The woman nodded. She and the boys said nothing but watched the group of men intently. Craig gave the command to go and the search team began its practised routine.

An hour later the section regrouped. Craig declared the all clear and the men clambered back into the two vehicles. The drive back seemed longer to Craig than the drive out. No one had the urge or the energy to speak. Craig scanned the sky for birds while Mick closed his eyes and dozed. Jock slept soundly, despite the bumpy journey.

That night Craig felt particularly restless. The wind had increased, stirring up the dust and making the tents heave and flap. He noticed himself straining to hear if anything sounded out of the ordinary. Listening to the swirl of the wind Craig fell asleep.

Everything was dark. He sensed something soft above his face. He couldn't move his arms or legs at all – not even turn his head. He could hear Angie's voice but he couldn't see her. His whole body was moving though, slowly, at a walking pace. Then suddenly he was floating, looking down – looking at himself, his body, shut in a coffin, on a hearse. Angie stood in the crowd. As the hearse drove past her, she spoke to him. He could see her but he couldn't hear what she said. She threw a white lily onto the hearse. She looked up. He looked down. Then he fell back into the dark.

Craig woke.

Three twenty-two a.m. according to his wristwatch. It was still dark, except for the low glow of security lights. Craig turned over and tried to get back to sleep.

The black feathers brushed across his cheek. Craig couldn't move his head. The raven hopped onto his forehead, its claws digging into his skull. 'Aark kraaak.' The raven's beak dipped. Craig woke.

'Krak, krak. Krak, krak, krak.' Small arms fired in the distance. Craig got up and went for a shower. Back at his tent he found a message to report to the platoon commander concerning new intelligence. Ten minutes later Craig arrived for the briefing.

'Morning Armstrong,' said the Lieutenant. 'I've got a rush task for your section.'

'Yes sir – what's the score?'

'That place you searched yesterday afternoon. Well, yesterday evening a Raven drone spotted several people moving back into the village after you'd gone. Looks like it might be a Taliban infiltration after all. Anyway, a Black Hawk's coming down at eleven hundred hours to have a nose about from the air. We need you to do a ground search again at the same time. Understood?'

'Yes sir. I'll get the boys kitted-up and ready for the off.'

'Good hunting Armstrong.'

'Thanks sir.'

Craig pulled his section together and briefed them. The two Land Rovers and their occupants left Patrol Base Blenheim at ten hundred hours precisely. The mail arrived at ten fifteen. One of the sappers put Angie's letter to Craig onto his bunk.

Dear Craig

I know I haven't written back to you for a while but I needed to sort myself out. The truth is that I've met someone else who I feel I want to be with more than you. Please don't take this news too hard and please don't try to contact me when you get back home.

I hope that one day you will see that it's best for both of us to break off now. I do hope one day you'll find someone who can love you better than me.

Angie

The two Land Rovers arrived at the edge of the village. This time there were no goats to be seen, nor any people. The men of Craig's section spread out to search the open areas around the houses first. Craig led three of the section on the search for improvised explosive devices, Jock nosing his way around busily with his head down, Mick following close behind him. The other four men scanned the fields and scrub for any sign of danger beyond the settlement. With his rifle slung over his left shoulder and his detector in his right hand, Craig could hear the heavy thudding of helicopter rotors getting louder and louder as the Black Hawk flew steadily towards them from the north.

The aircraft circled around the settlement, the down-draught from its rotors pushing dust and loose dirt into the air, forcing Craig's search and disposal team to stop their work. Jock ran under one of the Land Rovers and lay down. Then the helicopter wheeled away westwards to where a slight dust trail rising in the sky signalled vehicles on the move. Taliban? Not Craig's problem. His task was to finish searching and, if necessary, to clear the buildings in front of him.

With the Black Hawk gone, Jock emerged from under the Land Rover and padded up to Mick. Craig now moved his section on to phase two of the search operation – inside the houses. Four of the section remained on guard around the edge of the village while two teams of two men each took a building in turn – Mick and Steve, and Jock assisting, in one team, with Craig and Jon making up the other team. It would be slow work in the semi-darkness of the small houses.

Within minutes, Craig found a suspicious package – a medium-sized canvas bag laid against a wall behind a stool. He told Jon to leave the building while he examined it. Craig put down his detector and rifle. He heard Jon outside shouting to the others than they'd found an explosive device. Then all went quiet. He focused his attention on the bag, shining his torch to examine it better.

The bag was half open.

At the top was an old Nokia mobile phone with three wires, one red, one black, one blue, leading from the back of the phone into a yellow plastic container to which the phone was taped. Craig stood up. He'd seen a very similar device two months ago. Jock had sniffed it out and Mick had defused it, by cutting the blue wire. Blue – the colour of Angie's eyes.

'Aark, kraaak.' The sudden croak of a raven outside broke Craig's concentration. He listened as the bird hopped across the roof above him. He looked up. Then he heard another bird land next to the first, sending dust sprinkling down onto his face.

'Ark, aark, kraaak.' Craig rubbed his stinging eyes. He turned and took a step forward, away from the explosive device, towards the nearest door

– the small side door, not the main door he'd come in minutes earlier. The light from outside burned his dust-filled eyes.

'Aark, kraak.' Damn that bloody bird. Craig didn't see the thin wire as he stumbled through the opening.

The two related ballads, 'The Three Ravens' (Child 26/Roud 5) and 'Twa Corbies', have interested me for many years. First documented in the early seventeenth century (but likely older), 'The Three Ravens' is an English ballad in which a slain knight's hawk and hound protect his body from being despoiled by ravens until his beloved recovers his body and buries him, before dying herself. The 'chivalric' mood of 'The Three Ravens' contrasts starkly with the bleak realism of the Scottish 'Twa Corbies', in which the slain knight's hawk, hounds and 'lady fair' abandon him, leaving his body for the ravens to peck at, so that over his bare, white bones 'the wind shall blow for evermore'. I like to think of 'Twa Corbies' as a slightly later, cynical satire of 'The Three Ravens', with an originating context for both ballads possibly being some point during the Anglo-Scottish border wars of the thirteenth to sixteenth centuries. For my story I have conflated both ballads into a single narrative. For me, the central themes of loss, loyalty and love, so contrastingly represented in the two essentially medieval ballads, still resonate in our own time. I am also drawn to the ballads because I have deep ancestry on both sides of the Anglo-Scottish border, and it may well be that my forebears faced, and probably fought against, each other in that border region during the Middle Ages. I have chosen to adapt the ballads by setting my story in a near-contemporary military context – Afghanistan, around 2010. This is partly because I grew up myself in an armed forces background, living most of my childhood on military bases in the UK and abroad. It is also because I have first-hand experience, from childhood and more recently, of what living in a conflict zone is like.

18

The Migrant Maid

A Retelling of the Ballad 'King Cophetua and the Beggar Maid' by Anthony Nanson

Her arms across her breast she laid;
She was more fair than words can say:
Bare-footed came the beggar maid
Before the king Cophetua.

Alfred Lord Tennyson, 1833

It was not the best of times. Perhaps it wasn't the worst yet either. Ceaseless austerity. For some, ceaseless opportunity. Freed from the red tape of Brussels regulation, the Kingdom of England and Wales was a place apart. It was more than the world's biggest tax haven. It was a realm where those with the wherewithal could manufacture wealth out of nothing, out of less than nothing, by repackaging the debts of the world in layer after tottering layer of financial products. To those who have shall more be granted. The rich get richer and the poor get poorer.

On the helipad summit of the Corbett Tower in the City of London, Mr John W. Corbett trained his telescope across the canyon streets cutting between the office blocks. He was one of the ten per cent who owned ninety per cent. Or was it the five per cent who owned ninety-five per cent? It depends by which algorithm you compute as wealth the convoluted calculus of debt and risk. It pleased him to scan London's smog-blurred skyline and estimate through what arc he had to rotate the telescope to trace out a Euclidean sector equating to the proportion of the city's real estate that belonged to him.

The telescope was mounted on the simple rail at the roof's edge. Quite a place to jump. Not that Corbett was ever tempted; nothing of all that he owned would count for anything if he did not exist. He tilted the telescope to dive down through those gutter streets worth so much gold and paved with so much shit. When he clicked up the biotronic magnification he could see individual faces. It was his hobby to watch from this lofty height any person he found pleasing; to look, to admire, sometimes to strip them with his eye, without them ever knowing or returning his gaze; without any complication of connection. He could buy the pleasure of a sexy body whenever he wished. Money was no object. But in general he found it more satisfying just to look.

In the telescope's field of view a young woman's face caught his eye. She was sitting on the pavement, at the end of a row of beggars scrounging what they could till security moved them on. She had the long face and olive complexion of an Arab. The features were finely chiselled, very beautiful. The headscarfed head was held erect in spite of the abasement of her trade.

The telescope swooped on, but after a time Corbett's gaze returned along that street. The woman was still there. He looked and he looked. So many beautiful young women haunted the streets of London. What was it about this one? What was it that she had besides that lovely face? A serenity, an innocence? Something radiant from within.

Something that could not be had by looking.

Down there in the streets it was a muggy, stinky day in what they once called summer. The woman's bottom was sore from the hard pavement. Her skin itched beneath her unwashed clothes. Her belly ached with hunger. When a besuited young man came striding by she offered him her eyes and her practised half-smile, endured the brief appraisal before he reached in his pocket and a pair of coins clinked onto her begging cloth and her 'Allah yusallmak' was lost in the air behind him.

She glanced at the coins. That much nine times again and she could buy a cup of tea. What would her father have said if he'd seen her like this, smiling at men to solicit crumbs of their pity? By this means she could survive from one day to the next. But only just.

She was an illegal immigrant. She had no identity card, no address; no work was permitted her. Her father had made her dream of England. 'You study hard in school, girl, maybe you go to university there.' When their world had crashed down around them, and her brothers were taken by the war, he'd given her all the money the family could scrape together to ship her out of the country. It had got her as far as Cyprus, where she'd improved her English while she washed dishes and cleaned toilets, till the Turkish army overran the whole island and she'd had to flee again. When she finally got to England all she had left were the clothes on her back.

England was not what she'd imagined.

She no longer thought of the future, except for the hope of what comes beyond death.

Another man approached. Every line of his suit, his shoes, his haircut was oiled with the privilege of wealth. Rare it was to see a man like that in the street. Instead of speeding up to run the line of beggars, he slowed down. Her instinct because of that was to duck her face from his scrutiny. When she looked up he was slow-stepping past the others. She could feel the magnetic force dragging him. He turned.

A flurry of banknotes spilled onto the pavement.

Bonanza! There was a mad scramble. They were fifties! A couple of them and she could get a night in a hostel and wash her filthy body and her disgusting rags. Yet she dared not leap into the melee. And here was the rich man in front of her, looking at her.

'Don't be afraid,' he said.

Mr John W. Corbett saw that, though the woman was indeed beautiful and still young, her face was bone lean and prematurely lined by hardship and sorrow. The smell of her made him gag. Her garments were so threadbare that in places the skin showed through. Yet the quality he'd detected through the telescope, the inner beauty of her spirit, blazed from her, overwhelming now he stood before her, entrancing him.

'You're hungry, I think. Let me buy you some lunch.'

The woman's name was Zenelophon. She knew that men were drawn to her. In a moment like this, when a man overstepped the line of merely casting coins at her feet, her impulse was to run, hide, curl into a ball. But there was something about this man.

More than anything, it was an absence. An absence of need, of tension, of desire. And behind the grey eyes in his smooth, suntanned face was another kind of absence; a void that let her pity him.

There could be no question of her going into a restaurant in this filthy, stinky state. So it was to his apartment atop the Corbett Tower that he took her. Its opulence exceeded anything Zenelophon had ever seen or imagined. She spent an hour in the shining bathroom to soak out the grime engraved in her skin.

When, upon emerging, she saw the array of dresses, suits, lingerie he'd had bought for her, she wept. Never, even before the war, had she experienced such abundance. The food was nearly as overwhelming; more than two people could possibly eat. She wept at the thought of it going to waste.

'I'll have it given to the vagrants in the streets,' he said. 'Will that please you?'

He spoke as if she were not one of those unfortunates. Truly, she was one of them no longer.

In the days that followed, nothing she could want was denied her. Zenelophon knew it was her beauty that had won her this bounty. The sight of a smile on a pretty face was what she'd learnt to give and keep giving to survive; that and no more. She knew well the other way she could have sought to ease her hardship, but in all the trials of her flight from the wars, of the Kingdom's austerity, she had preserved her body's holiness. When Corbett understood she would not stay the night in his apartment, even in a room of her own, he ensconced her in a penthouse in one of his properties. He gave her more clothes and jewels and cosmetics. He bought ornaments to adorn her rooms. He sent a chauffeured car to bring her to dine with him in the perfumed, air-conditioned eateries to which only the privileged percentage had access.

Yet the weight of his wealth was smothering. Not merely the things he gave her, but the furnishings of his own residences, the sheer scale of his offices, the number and power of his cars and his copters, even the splendour of the food in the restaurants they ate in. Though she'd been given more than she'd ever dreamt of, she was not free. To return to the streets from which he'd rescued her was unthinkable. And as he talked about his businesses, answered her questions about them, and she began to learn how he creamed a profit from gambling with people's debts, even the debts of whole nations, it dawned upon her that millions of people across the world were held in bondage by their debts to him and people like him, though they knew it not. And Corbett knew it neither. For him it was only the arithmetic of business.

Nor was he free, could he have known it.

He perceived that what he admired in Zenelophon was something apart from the lovely things with which he adorned and surrounded her. Her beauty, of body and of soul, had been there when she was a beggar in the street and shone like a beacon amidst the leaden opulence of his private world. This alone was not his. And so his entrancement with her beauty evolved into a boldness to truly possess her, her body and her soul, and so win at last a return on his investment.

He laid his plans methodically. He ordered everything made ready at his most secluded property in Wales, an old farmhouse by a lake; he had the woods scoured of any squatters, or wandering migrants, or elderly romantics trespassing in search of refuge from the concrete, brick, and tarmac that had overrun the Kingdom; he instructed the security men to be discreet so it would seem the two of them were alone.

As they hiked down the path through the woods from the helipad he took Zenelophon's hand to guide her steps on the rough ground. Her face beamed with joy at the sunlight sparkling through the leaves and the music of birdsong bouncing between the trees.

'I had not known there was such a place in England! Or in the world! It is like the paradise that our storytellers made tales about and the scriptures remember and foretell.'

For once, in the lakeside cottage, he prepared the food with his own hands. She saw he was unpractised in that art and helped him. They laughed at their shared ineptitude in operating the cooker, but the food tasted all the better for the effort, so she said, and he agreed. Only when they'd eaten did she realise there was only the one bedroom – only the one bed.

'Mr Corbett —'

'"John" – please.'

'John ... in all that I've been through, all these years of destitution, I have never surrendered the honour that my mother and father impressed upon me and the Holy Scriptures teach.'

What a marvel in this day and age that a woman so beautiful should be untouched by a man! He would be tender. He would be kind. He fumbled for the words to tell her so.

'Do you not hear me, John Corbett? Must I speak crudely? Never have I *sold* my body, even in the hardest times when it seemed that would be the only way I could survive.'

'But —' He stopped short. She didn't need to spell out any more. That he'd sought to buy her. That, for all the generosity of what he'd given her, it was – to her – the same.

In the long silence the birdsong outside the cottage mocked them.

She said, 'John ... it is not that I do not like you. There is a beauty in you. A kindness. I think that I could love you. But I do not think you love me.'

What did she mean? What is love?

'Would you like me to marry you?' he said. 'So the antique laws of your faith will be respected? If that's what you want, I will marry you. Tonight. I'll copter in a registrar to do it.'

She shook her head. 'Still you would have bought me. Still you would not love me.'

'What then do you expect of me?'

She shrugged and once again she wept.

'Why are you crying, Zenelophon?'

'I'm weeping for the world; for all the millions of people who live in poverty, whose lives are as miserable as mine was. How can you love me if you don't love them?'

Back in London, Corbett vented his frustration in a frenzy of charity. He drove through the streets flinging wads of banknotes from the window. There were scuffles, near riots, to grab them. It was viral in the media. Crowds of people thronged in the City in hopes of more. He gave away so much money that prices in London inflated.

'What really changes when you give charity?' demanded Zenelophon. 'Still the people are not free. And in your own companies your executives earn ten thousand times more than the women who clean your office floors.'

So he called in his accountants and his human resources directors. They went over the numbers. They argued, of course. They thought he was mad. Most of them had left before the changes were made. But others came to replace them. When the pay multiplier of ten thousand was reduced to ten, the highest salaries were still adequate to live in style, and the men and women willing to take them were a new breed of executive. They did the work because they enjoyed it. They worked more efficiently. They could be trusted. And because the Corbett Group was so large what happened there had an impact on other firms. The lowest paid wanted to be paid more. The owners cottoned on to the saving that could be made when the highest paid were paid less.

He talked it all through with Zenelophon. She became his business counsellor and conscience. The promise of her diligence in her long-lost schooldays blossomed into an astuteness of insight and curiosity. Always she asked questions. Why do they do this? Whose well-being does this serve? Her mind boggled at the castles in the sky erected by his companies' financial products, and how they amplified the transfer of wealth to the rich at the cost of the toil of the world's poor and what was left of the world's ecology. The impulses of Corbett's new executives travelled the same paths as Zenelophon's Socratic questions: their enthusiasm was for the real work – for the portfolios in renovation and rebuilding, in farming and food production, in shipbuilding, pharmaceuticals, microgeneration, and renewables.

It came to a head one lunchtime when Corbett arrived outside Zenelophon's residence to find her on the pavement with an armful of fine clothes he'd given her. She was giving them away, to vagrants, migrants, whatever they were – scrawny, sallow women, some of them jabbering with her in Arabic.

'What are you doing? Those are *yours*!'

'If they are mine, they're mine to give away. They're more than I need. I am happy in this.' A plain blue dress and a paler blue headscarf, whose simplicity only magnified the beauty of the one who wore them.

They sat down to coffee and the argument continued. She tutored him with her zeal. They looked together from the window and her arm pressed warm upon his as she drew his gaze to the people down there in the street. He needed no telescope to see what she saw: the humanity of each one of them, each one a precious soul like her, however low they'd been driven.

He understood what her questions had compelled him to see: that the trade in repackaged debt had driven the majority of the world's people into poverty, given traction to violence in the struggle to survive, stripped resources from land and sea without replenishing them. One thing was needed above all: an end to that trade, to the options, swaps, and futures, the hedging, dealing, and speculation.

The government was toothless to do it. What, though, if one of the big players took unilateral action? What if he, John W. Corbett, were to write off all the tangled tiers of debt he controlled? What chain reaction might that trigger if each link in the world's web of being is connected to every other? It would suck his assets dry. He'd have to liquidise his real estate. He'd have nothing left except his businesses that produced tangible products and services that people really needed. When he'd paid all the salaries he'd barely break even. He'd be no richer than his employees. Give your riches to the poor and follow me. Would he do that to win this woman's love? Would she love him because he'd done it? Or would he do it because he loved her and she'd made him love the world?

My adaptation of 'King Cophetua and the Beggar Maid' takes inspiration from Burne-Jones's painting based on Tennyson's poem of the same story, and art critics Martin Harrison and Bill Waters' interpretation of the painting as concerned with 'renunciation of material wealth for an idea of beauty' and 'the erosion of spiritual values by worldly considerations'. These themes seem to me even more salient today than they were in the nineteenth century. The original ballad is in Thomas Percy's Reliques of Ancient English Poetry *(George Bell, 1765).*

19

The Two Visitors

A Retelling of the Ballad 'The Twa Magicians'/ 'The Coal Black Smith' by Kevan Manwaring

She turnd hersell into a ship,
To sail out ower the flood;
He ca'ed a nail intill her tail,
And syne the ship she stood.

ANON

Sunita Jadugar ('Sunny' to her ESA team mates) gazed at the blizzard of the monitor, frowning. A second ago she was sure she had seen a ... what? ... A shadow, a shape? ... appear briefly out of the visual static. But all there was now was the endless snowstorm that had bedevilled her monitor for hours. Her instruments had not been working properly since she had come into orbit around the moon. She tilted her head to look out through the cupola. Her eyes relayed information which her brain was still questioning, but there it was: the largest moon in the solar system, Ganymede, darkly cracked and icy and, beneath the frozen surface, chthonic oceans – a glimmer beneath the skull. The JUICE mission had confirmed what they had all hoped for – evidence of water, more than all of Earth's oceans combined, and with it, the possibility of life.

The proof of life on other planets would take the pressure off the fragile miracle of Earth with its too many people and too few resources. If life could exist elsewhere then humankind had a second shot.

Did it deserve one? Sunny pondered. At times, the infinite silence and darkness of space made her melancholic. Sometimes she looked out of the cupola and saw nothing at all. No hope, no meaning.

But today – the mission went by Lunar Base Time – all of that had changed. For months Ganymede had been a speck in their most powerful telescope, a blot on the face of Jupiter. Once dwarfed by the gas giant's red eye, now it filled Jadugar's field of vision. Her Punjabi features were transposed onto it in the viewing window's reflection.

Her mother, her father, would have been so proud. They had taught her to look up, to behold the stars, to wonder at the myriad possibilities they held. How far she had come, how far.

It had been a lonely haul since separating from the mother ship, *Hera*. She piloted one of the three scout crafts – one for each of the three of the four Galilean moons scheduled to be explored, Europa, Callisto, and Ganymede, named after their respective destinations. Io, the driest known object in the solar system, and a volcanic hell, was a non-starter. Of course, she kept in touch whenever their respective orbits would allow – precious windows of human contact. Hearing the voices of her fellow expedition members kept her sane. By herself, alone, millions of miles from home, the vastness of space pressing in around her. Sometimes she found it soothing, meditative – playing some ambient music as she attended to a task – but today it was making her jittery. She was starting to hear things – voices in the static – and, lately, see things.

She scanned back through the monitor's data. There. Yes, a distinct shape. She played it on a loop. There was no mistaking it. A shadow in the light. A humanoid one. She shuddered as though an icy hand had suddenly caressed her. She could feel something watching her.

Looking up, she saw, beyond the cupola, the dark silhouette of a man, or something like one, staring back at her.

He, and it was definitely a he, was naked, chiselled, muscles delineated as though cast in bronze. His skin writhed with power: obsidian shot through with lightning – a negative of the firestorms raging on Jupiter. His eyes burnt with the intense spectrum of a forge. Then he reached out a hand, and pressed it up against the glass, close enough for her to see the luminescent labyrinths of his fingerprints.

An aureole of sparks extended his touch, furnace spunks seeking access.

Jadugar froze in terror as the thing lent closer – gazing, scrutinizing, leering at her. Those forge-eyes penetrated to her very soul. And then he smiled, his teeth as red as the Eye.

Jadugar recoiled, kicking herself away from the cupola and somersaulting with practised grace. Kicking off from the opposite side, she launched herself along the main shaft of her ship, sleek but vulnerable in her skin-tight base-suit.

All her instincts screamed run. But first she had to send a message. She had to warn the others. She pushed herself along, the zero-gs working with her, giving her speed, but not enough. It was like flying through treacle, swimming in quicksand. Ganymede had the seventh highest gravity in the solar system. Was it starting to affect the craft?

She reached the comms and quickly opened the message channel. 'This is Jadugar, Ganymede. There is something out there. It is attacking the ship. It's …'

The comms fizzed and sparked.

He was before her. He was *inside*. The intruder must have been at least seven foot tall, his dark frame sucking in all the light. Forked lightning crackled across his broad frame.

He opened his arms as if to embrace her.

Jadugar reacted physically before even being able to think of a response. She'd had enough training to know how to defend herself, both in armed and unarmed combat. Sliding out of his grasp, she used the nearest available weapon – the fire extinguisher. Snapping out the pin, she fired it into his face, into the furnace of his eyes, momentarily blinding him. The force shot her across the command deck.

The controls were going haywire. Everything was blinking red. The system alarm brayed in her head, making it hard to think. As the intruder swept his arms around in an arc, the panels went out one by one, as though the shadow of an eclipse passed over them. Suddenly the ship was plunged into red light, the emergency back-up kicking in.

The *Ganymede* was dying.

Lucid in a crisis after years of training and preparation, Jadugar knew immediately what she had to do. She made for the dock. Inexorable as a shadow, the darkness followed her. Sweat beading from her face, floating away as she spun this way and that, she made it to the suit locker, hit the button to open it, screaming at the slow hydraulics.

Two red eyes. Twin Jupiters. Getting closer. No time. He'd been on her in seconds. She could hear the calm voice of her Canadian instructor, back in Star City. 'Work the problem.'

In a flash she knew the denouement of this. Punched the control panel, lit up in the half-light. She palmed it. Issued the command: initiate de-pressurisation. The countdown began. Ten. Nine. The suit locker slowly opened. Eight. Seven. Finally, she could slide in. Six. Five. Close it up. Four. Three. Helmet. 'Lock into place dammit!' Two. Gloves. Left. One. Right.

The forge eyes were before her. The red mouth. The storm inside, threatening to engulf her. Hands crackled, reaching for her ungainly body. A blast of light, rushing wind. A point of singularity into which everything was sucked. The intruder – flushed away. A red scream, until that was taken too. Jadugar tried to hang on – wedging herself against the side of the locker. But. She. Could. Not. Hang. On. Forever. Her strength went. She was sucked out of the airlock.

Floating, in the vast darkness. Spinning, amid all the flotsam and jetsam. The cold eye of Ganymede watching over her. Sliding in and out of vision – her ship. Spinning away, like a misfiring firework.

All hope lost.

No one would get her out of this. What was it her father used to say? 'Always paddle your own canoe.' She looked around at the evacuated contents of her ship. There must be something. Work the problem, girl.

Her small black idol of Ganesha floated past her, hiding stars as it gyrated. Her teammates had ribbed her at her 'lucky gonk'. A sentimental keepsake of home. But, in this moment, so much more. There. The EVA pack. If she could reach it. There were small jets on her suit. Good for short blasts only. Limited power. Just enough to steer her in the right direction. She lined herself up. The angle had to be just right. Then, occluding her view of the EVA – a dark figure.

The intruder. Between her and the pack. She had to risk it. No other way. It'll be like a schoolyard game. The bully in her way, waiting to give her a beating if she came close.

Jadugar gritted her teeth. Fired the jets.

Shot like a rocket towards the waiting arms of the intruder. Arc-light crackled between his hands. At the last minute, she fired her jets again. Dodged his deadly grip by millimetres. 'Not today, Mister Sparks.'

Last burst. No second chances. She hurtled towards the EVA. Closer. Closer. Red eyes in pursuit. She reached out with all her might. 'Come on!' she screamed. A dark shadow behind her. Her gloved hand brushed a stray strap of the EVA pack. She flailed, grabbed it, pulled it, pulled it closer.

He was nearly within reach. She grabbed the joystick, punched the controls to fire it up. Held on, as the thrusters shot her away from her pursuer. She could barely keep a grip, dragged along by the rocketing pack, a white block of power. The black shadow followed. Relentless. She couldn't outrun him for long like this. Jadugar pulled herself with all her strength into the arms of the pack, clipped herself in. Blasted away from the being. 'Eat thruster!'

Heart beating wildly, she tried to breathe slower, ease herself into the grace of flight. At first, as she regained control, the jink-jinking was accidental – but that was enough to buy her time. Then, zen. Like back in the training pool. Steady the breathing. Don't use up all your oxygen.

Faces looking at her from above the water line, blurred, all integrity of outline lost. Changing shape. As she had to. Adapt to survive. She soared away from him, it, whatever it was. Back towards the ship, spinning dangerously out of control, losing orbit. It was too late to save it. The moon had caught it in its deadly riptide. But there was something aboard that could save her. She steered herself to the life-pod attached to one end. It was little more than a sarcophagus, designed purely for re-entry. Entering the vessel was hard – as it spun out of control. She had to hold her nerve. And all the while – the nightmare at her back. Calm. Breathe.

A silent prayer to an old god. With a well-timed blast, she was inside. She ditched the pack, and floated along to the pod. Activated it. Lightning crackled in the darkened craft. The moon looming in and out of view. Everything going haywire. Flowers of fire in the dark. She slipped into the pod, sealed it. The launch sequence kicked in. She prayed that it would not malfunction – its systems independent of the ship.

The forge-eyes glaring at her. The hands of lightning. Blast off. The pod was jettisoned in a blur of intense g-force. Through the tiny window she saw the *Ganymede* explode. No way home. Only down.

The life-pod began its descent, and her world became continuous vibration. Outside, the glare of intense heat. She was a shooting star. All was light, noise, motion. Her mother singing: 'You are my sunshine'. Then, blocking the light – the dark face. Holding on, somehow. The g-forces, the heat, blended, melted, stretched the figure; yet still it clung on, crackling with power. It became a thin hide, a parachute of skin.

Jadugar passed out as the life-pod smashed through the icy surface, its intense heat melting a smooth passage through into the subterranean ocean below. At the last moment the emergencies thrusters fired to slow her terminal velocity. The pod smashed down like the gavel of a High Court judge.

Somehow, she was not in smithereens. Her craft, her vertebrae, were intact. Part of Sunny's brain registered the cold fact: splashed down in the icy waters of Ganymede. The ripples of her impact subsided. The folds of the chute, crumpled leeward, and tangled up in them, the intruder, limp, but not quite life-less.

'Sunny.'

A voice calling. Her father's?

'Wake up, slug-a-bed.'

She regained consciousness. Water, or something like it, slapped against the window of the sarcophagus. A whole dark ocean of it. Far above, the exit wound of her arrival through the ice, stars glittering, remote, unattainable, beyond. Sensors informed her of what she could not believe. She had survived. And here she was, inside Ganymede.

She made a silent prayer to the anima mundi: *may we learn from you, and not merely take.* The pod had a stellar sail, provisions and, if all else failed, a paddle. She pulled in the chute, hauling in her catch like a fisherman. The intruder was a flimsy ribbon of limbs, spluttering, quenched. This was her hammer now. She would harness its power, she would learn from it, and she would survive.

But then, as she looked at the sentient being laying prone before her, exhausted, vulnerable, a man of stars fallen into an abyss, she thought again. Hadn't such primitive instincts and inclinations got them into this position in the first place? Here she was, the first human on a new world, the conquering colonist, and the cycle could start all over again. Or not. She had a choice.

The alien, the other alien, began to stir. Sunny made a decision. She would learn its language, or teach it her's, and on this strange moon, beneath the stars and ice, they would start to tell each other their stories.

I chose the problematic ballad of 'The Two Magicians' ('The Twa Magicians' or 'The Coal Black Smith', Child 44/Roud 1350), as a creative challenge and as an illustration of what could be called the 'Ballad Tale' process, which frees up both the author and the material. How to reconstruct such a ballad? There are many songs in the folk tradition that depict the status between men and women unevenly, perpetuate negative images of women, of motherhood, of the empowered female operating under her own agency. Rather than reinforce their questionable subtexts, the conscious practitioner should surely seek to subvert, challenge or transform such material. This is not to bowdlerise ballads, turning them into anaemic, neutered shadows of their former selves, Disneyfied and disembowelled. With a little bit of ingenuity it is possible to repurpose even

*the most misogynistic or morally suspect of songs (leaving extant versions as
important if repugnant artefacts of social history). Perhaps this is easier for
the ballad-tale writer, than the ballad-singer, although many such rework-
ings have succeeded in song, even if it is through the cadence of the singer or
the arrangement which transforms the tone and thus ironic distance of the
performer to the material. There are several different versions of the song, originating from at least two known sources (my favourite being via Nancy Thym
on 'If I had Wings Like Noah's Dove'. Nancy cited her source as a blacksmith
named, perfectly, 'Mr Sparks', of Minehead, Somerset, who sang it to her on
8 August 1904). Many famous, and less famous, folkies have had a crack at
it – Bert Lloyd, Martin Carthy, Dave Swarbrick, Bellowhead, et al. I first
came to know the song, as most did, through Steeleye Span's lusty 1974 version
on Now We Are Six (and I used its opening lines to jumpstart my version:
'She looked out of the window as white as any milk/And he looked in at the
window as black as any silk'). It is hard to get that jaunty tune out of your
head, but the Dovetail Trio have done a good job with their 2015 version.
They dug out some new verses, including:*

Then she became a star, a star all in the night
And he became a thundercloud and muffled her out of sight

*The variant chains of transformations are fascinating. The Child 44 ver-
sion is perhaps the most thorough: turtle dow/another dow; eel/speckled trout;
duck/drake; hare/greyhound; grey mare/gilt saddle; het girdle/cake; ship/
nail; silken plaid/green covering. Yet strip away all of this fith-fathing and
essentially what you have is a chase, and a game of brinkmanship – one that
is foreshadowed in many myths and legends (Arne-Thompson tale types 333
& 325). A.L. Lloyd, in his 1966 sleeve-notes on the track, saw it in the early
Indian myth-cycle:*

In Hindu scripture, when the first man pursued the first woman, she
thought to hide by changing into a cow, but he became a bull and so cattle
were born. She turned into a mare and he into a stallion, she a jenny and
he a jackass, ewe and ram, on and on till all the world was created, down
to the ants.

Unaware of this initially, I had made my protagonist an Indian astronaut. For me, this confirmed I had got back to their quintessence of the ballad. But, of course, I have my resourceful heroine come out on top in the end, to completely subvert the power discourse. Sunny is just as much a magician as 'Mr Sparks', as her surname, Jadugar, suggests (Jaadoogar is Punjabi for 'magician'). As the writer, I have, in my small way, joined this company of enchanters, adding to the layers of transformation with my lateral adaptation. It does not 'break' the original, if indeed one can be traced. The seed is already amongst us — and has been for millennia. We are a hybrid breed, born of stardust and mud.

The Contributors

NIMUE BROWN grew up with folk music and ran a club in the Midlands for about a decade. She sings and plays the bouzouki. Nimue has written a number of speculative novels, including the graphic novel series *Hopeless Maine*, and is colourist on the John Matthews/ Tom Brown graphic novel adaptation of *Le Morte D'Arthur*. She has some Pagan non-fiction titles with Moon Books and blogs most days at Druid Life – book reviews feature regularly. Walking, reading, barding, crafting and contemplating take up what little spare time remains.

PETE CASTLE was born and brought up in Ashford, Kent. He went to Bretton Hall College of Education in Yorkshire in 1965 where he met his wife Sue and then taught for ten years before going professional as a folk singer in 1978. In the early 1980s he discovered oral storytelling and started to do the two in tandem, which he has done ever since. Pete and Sue moved to Derbyshire in 1987 and now live in Belper. Pete has a great fondness for story songs and has sung many of the 'big ballads' over the years. Since 1999 he has edited *Facts & Fiction* storytelling magazine and is the author of three books of Folk Tales for The History Press.

CHRISSY DERBYSHIRE is a writer, folklorist and storyteller living in Wales. Her first collection, *Mysteries*, was published by Awen Publications in 2008. Since then she has contributed to several collections, journals and magazines. In 2014 her story 'Sovay, Sovay' was featured in Honno Press's *The Wish Dog and Other Stories: Haunting Tales from Welsh Women Writers*. Two of her stories have been chosen for the upcoming independent TV series *Fragments of Fear*, a spooky adult *Jackanory*.

FIONA EADIE is passionate about language and about bringing the spoken word to life. Like most storytellers, she works with stories that have come down through the oral tradition and tells these in schools, museums, arts centres and at weddings and music/literature festivals. She runs a monthly 'Storytelling Saturday' session at Ruskin Mill in Gloucestershire and occasional 'Introduction to Storytelling' workshops. Fiona also devises storywalks through particular landscapes and creates or revives stories of place for, among others, the Lichfield Festival and the National Trust.

MALCOLM GREEN loves the wild things of this world, weaving his knowledge and experience of the earth and its life into his tales. He is an experienced educator and workshop leader, teaching at Newcastle University, running courses all over the world and working in schools. He is a founder member of A Bit Crack North East Storytelling, one of the longest-running storytelling groups in the country, which has been presenting monthly storytelling events, festivals and cutting-edge storytelling projects for over twenty-five years. He is interested in the role storytelling has in creating a more sustainable way of living.

KIRSTY HARTSIOTIS is a Gloucestershire-based storyteller and writer. She has performed widely in Britain and beyond, and with storytelling company Fire Springs, has co-produced ecobardic epics such as *Arthur's Dream*, *Robin of the Wildwood*, and *Return to Arcadia*. She is the author of *Wiltshire Folk Tales*, *Suffolk Folk Tales*, *Gloucestershire Ghost Tales* (co-author) and *Suffolk Ghost Tales* (co-author – forthcoming 2017). She has worked in the heritage industry for more than twenty years as a curator and educator, and came to storytelling with a lifelong love of stories and the histories and places that inform them.

MARK HASSALL works as a psychological therapist with children and young people and has an interest in using traditional storytelling in his therapeutic work and in the local community. He lives with his family between Dartmoor and the South Devon coast.

SIMON HEYWOOD is the author of *The Legend of Vortigern* (The History Press, 2012), *South Yorkshire Folk Tales* (with Damien Barker, The History Press 2014), and several articles, poetry, and translations. He has toured nationally and internationally as a storyteller, delivering commissions for Festival at the Edge and the Beyond the Border International Storytelling Festival. He won Best Collaboration at the 2012 British Awards for Storytelling Excellence for 'Gilgamesh' with Tim Ralphs, and Best Documentary at the 2005 Strasbourg Film Festival for *Contempt of Conscience* with Joe Jenkins. His songs and music have been recorded, performed and broadcast by Albireo, Crucible, Melrose Quartet, and others.

ALAN M. KENT was born in St Austell, Cornwall. He studied at the Universities of Cardiff and Exeter, gaining a doctorate in Cornish and Anglo-Cornish Literature. He was a Lecturer in Literature for the Open University in South-West Britain and a Visiting Fellow in Celtic Studies at the University of Coruña, Galicia. He wrote award-winning novels, poems and plays. His most recent publications include *National Minority* (2015), *Interim Nation* (2015) and *Dan Daddow's Cornish Comicalities* (2016). He was series editor of *Lesser Used Languages of Europe* and *Cornish and Celtic Alternatives*. Alan died due to a short illness in July 2022.

ANDY KINNEAR is a printmaker working in screen print, letterpress and woodcut. His prints can be viewed as individual pieces, but in combination they form a narrative. His inspiration comes from eighteenth-century broadside prints, twentieth-century poster design and magical realist literature. He obtained a MA with distinction in printmaking from The University of the West of England in 2013 and has a BA in Fine Art.

THE CONTRIBUTORS

LAURA KINNEAR has had short stories published in *PenPusher* and the *Stroud Short Stories* anthology and was longlisted for the Fish Short Story Prize. She works as a Museum Curator and is currently redrafting her first novel.

Australian-born **ERIC MADDERN** came to live in Britain aged eleven. Later he made a ten-year journey around the world, culminating in work as a bush artist in the Aboriginal communities of Central Australia. Since then he's lived in Snowdonia, North Wales, where he's created, with others, the Cae Mabon Eco-Retreat Centre. He is now a storyteller, author (writings include children's picture books and *Snowdonia Folk Tales*) and singer-songwriter. His recent albums are *Full of Life* and *Rare and Precious Earth*. He's an 'honorary chief bard' in OBOD and for over twenty years has explored the 'Matter of Britain' in retreats for storytellers with Hugh Lupton.

KEVAN MANWARING was co-founder of Fire Springs, with whom he performed in many storytelling shows, as well as in the duo Brighid's Flame. These days he is Senior Lecturer in Creative Writing at Arts University Bournemouth. He is the author of *Turning the Wheel*, *Desiring Dragons*, *The Long Woman*, *Lost Islands*, and editor of *Heavy Weather: tempestuous tales of stranger climes* (The British Library) as well as collections of folk tales for The History Press. He blogs and tweets as the Barbaric Academic, and is a regular contributor to BBC Radio 3's 'Free Thinking'.

CANDIA MCKORMACK was born in Stroud and grew up in one of Gloucestershire's Severnside villages. She formed the Gothic Pagan band Inkubus Sukkubus with her now husband Tony McKormack in 1989, while they were both studying Graphic Design in Gloucester. The band is still going strong, having just released their twenty-first album, and they continue to write songs inspired by witchcraft, the supernatural world, and the folklore of the British Isles. Candia is also deputy editor of *Cotswold Life* magazine.

DAVID METCALFE is a narrative consultant, writer, performance storyteller and folk singer. He is particularly interested in narrative interpretation of landscape, archaeology and history, in the impact of humankind on landscape evolution, and in human communities' interactions with each other. His oral storytelling and folk singing draw mainly on the rich indigenous traditions of the British Isles. David believes that storytelling practice has broad application in life – that, as well as being performance art and entertainment, it can inspire transformation in people and make a beneficial contribution in areas such as lifelong learning, psychological well-being, organisational improvement and personal development.

ANTHONY NANSON has performed internationally as a story-teller and co-produced, with Fire Springs, such ecobardic epics as *Arthur's Dream*, *Robin of the Wildwood*, *Return to Arcadia*, and *Dark Age Deeds of the Celtic Saints*. His books include *Exotic Excursions*, *Storytelling and Ecology*, *Storytelling for a Greener World* (co-editor), *Gloucestershire Ghost Tales* (co-author), award-winning *Gloucestershire Folk Tales* and *Words of Re-enchantment*, and the novel *Deep Time*. Anthony teaches creative writing at Bath Spa University and runs the ecobardic small press Awen Publications. A love of nature, authenticity, and the spirit of place informs all his work.

DAVID PHELPS returned to his native Herefordshire after a career in the civil service to research and tell stories from his native county. He is the author of four books, *Herefordshire Folk Tales, Haunted Hereford, The Bloody History of Hereford* and *Worcestershire Folk Tales*, all published by The History Press. He now lives on the Herefordshire/Worcestershire border with his partner, the storyteller Valerie Dean. In his spare time he tends an allotment and if anyone would like some free-range (and well-fed) slugs he would be happy to oblige.

KAROLA RENARD was born in Germany and moved to the UK in 2009. A journalist, editor and translator, she published her first collection of short fiction in 2011 (*The Firekeeper's Daughter*, Awen). She lives in Devon with her husband and young daughter.

RICHARD SELBY is a storyteller, writer, and bookseller with a keen interest in modern art and modern poetry. He performs solo as a storyteller, with Fire Springs and occasionally with musician Beth Porter. *The Fifth Quarter* – his collection of prose, poetry, and tales about Romney Marsh in Kent – was published in 2008. *The Mouth of the Night* followed in 2012 and his new book of poetry *The Marsh* with illustrations by Nigel Davison is due for publication this winter. He lives in Bath with his wife Judith and has family associations with Romney Marsh which go back 100 years.

CHANTELLE SMITH is a folk singer based in North Wiltshire. Her particular area of interest is performing traditional ballads and creating versions that are accessible to modern audiences from the various (and varied) versions of the old ballads that have been recorded over the past few centuries. Chantelle is currently working on her first solo EP. As well as singing traditional folk songs on her own, Chantelle also performs as a member of contemporary folksinger/songwriter Talis Kimberley's band, and also in the folk song/storytelling duo Bríghid's Flame with Kevan Manwaring.

Select Bibliography

Books

Key works

Bishop, Julia & Steve Roud (eds), *The New Penguin Book of English Folk Song* (Allen Lane, 2012)

Bronson, Bertrand, *The Traditional Tunes of the Child Ballads*, 4 vols (Princeton University Press, 1959-1972) (Loomis House Press edition includes audio recordings on CD)

Buchan, David, *The Ballad and the Folk* (Routledge, 1972)

Child, Francis James (ed.), *The English and Scottish Popular Ballads*, vols 1-5, various editions

Morrish, John (ed.), *The Folk Handbook: Working with Songs from the English Tradition* (Backbeat Books, 2007)

Percy, Thomas, *Reliques of Ancient English Poetry* (George Bell & Sons, 1876)

Roud, Steve, *Folk Song in England* (Faber, 2017)

Scott, Walter, *Minstrelsy of the Scottish Borders*, various editions (the 2016 Edinburgh Edition, edited by Professor Sigrid Rieuwerts is the most authoritative)

Sharp, Cecil J. (ed.), *One Hundred English Folk Songs: For Medium Voice* (Dover Song Collections, 1976)

Background works

Andersen, F.G., Holzapfel, O. and Pettitt, T., *The Ballad as Narrative: Studies in the Ballad Traditions of England, Scotland, Germany and Denmark* (Odense: Odense University Press, 1982)

Atkinson, D. and Roud, S., *Street Ballads in Nineteenth-Century Britain, Ireland, and North America: The Interface between Print and Oral Traditions* (Ashgate, 2014)

Boyes, G., *The Imagined Village: culture, ideology and the English Folk Revival* (Manchester University Press, 1993)

Coffin, T.P., *The British Traditional Ballad in North America* (University of Texas Press, 1977)

Fox Strangways, A.H. (in collaboration with Maud Karpeles), *Cecil Sharp* (OUP, 1933)

Hustvedt, S.B., *Ballad Books and Ballad Men: Raids and Rescues in Britain, America, and the Scandinavian North since 1800* (Harvard University Press, 1930)

Websites

www.vwml.org – The Vaughan Williams Memorial Library Catalogue, where you can access the Roud Index online

www.sacred-texts.com – A full list of English and Scottish popular ballads by Francis James Child can be found here

Society *for* Storytelling

Since 1993, the Society for Storytelling has championed the art of oral storytelling and the benefits it can provide – such as improving memory more than rote learning, promoting healing by stimulating the release of neuropeptides, or simply great entertainment! Storytellers, enthusiasts and academics support and are supported by this registered charity to ensure the art is nurtured and developed throughout the UK.

Many activities of the Society are available to all, such as locating storytellers on the Society website, taking part in our annual National Storytelling Week at the start of every February, purchasing our quarterly magazine *Storylines*, or attending our Annual Gathering – a chance to revel in engaging performances, inspiring workshops, and the company of like-minded people.

You can also become a member of the Society to support the work we do. In return, you receive free access to *Storylines*, discounted tickets to the Annual Gathering and other story-telling events, the opportunity to join our mentorship scheme for new storytellers, and more. Among our great deals for members is a 30% discount off titles in the *Folk Tales* series from The History Press website.

For more information, including how to join, please visit

www.sfs.org.uk